MW00907002

TROUBLE AT THE ANIMAL SHELTER

A Cedar Bay Cozy Mystery - Book 11

BY

DIANNE HARMAN

Published by: Dianne Harman
www.dianneharman.com

Interior, cover design and website by
Vivek Rajan
wwwYourMissingLinks.com

ISBN: 978-1541267176

CONTENTS

ACKNOWLEDGMENTS

To You, My Readers:

Thank you for buying and borrowing my books. I appreciate you reaching out to me time and again with suggestions and letting me know what you like about my books, and occasionally, what you don't like. I carefully review all of the input I receive from you. I know your time is valuable, and I truly appreciate you taking time to share your thoughts with me.

I would be remiss if I didn't thank you for the time you take from your busy schedules to read my books. That is the biggest gift I can be given, and I want you to know how much it's appreciated by me.

As always, a special thank you to Vivek and Tom. Vivek, for providing such beautiful book covers, sound advice, and the ability to make the technical parts of publishing a book look easy. Tom, for your support, suggestions, being my best friend, and sharing your life with me for so many years!

Win FREE Paperbacks every week!

Go to www.dianneharman.com/freepaperback.html and get your FREE copies of Dianne's books and favorite recipes immediately by signing up for her newsletter.

Once you've signed up for her newsletter you're eligible to win three paperbacks. One lucky winner is picked every week. Hurry before the offer ends!

DIANNE HARMAN

PROLOGUE

When he turned the corner in his black and white Beaver County patrol car, Deputy Brandon Wynn saw the flames and smoke coming from the house. He radioed the fire department dispatch operator and reported the fire as he pulled up in front of the house. A few moments later Fire Chief Wayne Rogers radioed him back requesting further details about the fire.

"Chief, got a fire in an old farmhouse on the west side of town on Cinder Street. Looks like it's just getting started. I don't have the exact address, but you won't be able to miss it. Just look for the big column of smoke. Better hurry," he said as he pressed the don't talk button on his radio.

Wouldn't you know it. I thought tonight would be a slow night and now this. Well, fires are the chief's concern, not mine. I just want to make sure no one's trapped inside the house. The woman who called said she heard a lot of dogs barking at the house in question, but she sure didn't say anything about a fire.

When he opened his patrol car door he heard a number of dogs frantically barking, and from the sound of them, they were still in the house. Brandon raced up to the front door, pulled on the doorknob, and threw it open. Dogs of every breed, size, and type ran out of the house. He stood looking in amazement, not believing what he was seeing. He estimated at least thirty dogs had been in the house. Fortunately, the big yard of the old farmhouse was fenced, so none

1

of them escaped.

A fire truck roared up the street just as he was placing a call to the Cedar Bay Animal Shelter director, Jenna Lee, to have people come and round up the dogs. When the fire truck came to a stop, members of the four-man crew jumped out and within ten minutes they had the fire extinguished. The firemen walked into the house to make sure there weren't any hot spots left. A moment later one of the firemen hurried out of the house and yelled, "Deputy, you better come here. Looks like there may have been a reason for this fire."

Brandon followed the fireman inside. He motioned for Brandon to follow him down the hall. When they entered a bedroom at the end of the hall he saw a white-haired woman's body lying on the bed in a pool of blood. There was a large bullet hole in the center of her chest. He walked over to her, but there was no reason to check for a pulse. She was obviously dead. He gently pulled her eyelids over her eyes, knowing she would never see anything again.

He turned to the fireman that had led him to the bedroom and said as he walked out of the room, "There's a good chance the fire was deliberately started by whoever murdered that poor woman in the bedroom. Probably hoped the fire would destroy any evidence of the crime. Have your men treat the fire as arson and start looking for evidence. I need to make a couple of calls."

A few minutes later a woman approached him as he was walking down the hall and said, "Brandon, what's going on? There must be over thirty dogs running loose in the yard. I don't know where we'll put all of them. The shelter's almost at capacity as it is," Jenna Lee, the director of the shelter, said.

"Jenna, I have no idea. You know as much as I do. Can you round up the dogs and take them to the shelter for now? Maybe you can get some volunteers to place them in foster homes for a few days until all of this gets sorted out."

"Sure. I'll see what I can do. I brought the only van we have, and I'm going to have to make a number of trips to get all of them transported to the shelter. One of my helpers came with me, and we brought a lot of leashes. We'll get started immediately." She walked away, unaware that a woman had been murdered and was in the next room.

Brandon pressed in Mike Reynolds' telephone number on his cell phone. Mike was the sheriff of Beaver County and the one who would be overseeing the murder investigation. "Mike, hate to ruin your evening, but it looks like we've got a murder on our hands." He told him what he and the fireman had found as well as the problem of getting the dogs to the shelter.

"You and Kelly will be here as soon as you can? Good. Jenna could use some help. There's dogs everywhere you look. It's a real mess. See you in a few."

CHAPTER ONE

"Kelly, I'm still not real clear on how visiting a nursing home with a dog works. I thought they weren't allowed in places like that, although I'd think any nursing home would be honored to have these three come and visit," he said as he looked down at the dogs lying at his feet.

Rebel, the fawn colored big boxer Kelly owned before she'd married Mike a couple of years ago, was clearly the alpha dog of the group. On one side of him was Lady, a yellow Lab that Mike had given Kelly right before they were married, and on the other side of him was Skyy, a German shepherd puppy given to them after the owner of the Doggie Love Kennel had been murdered.

Kelly reached down and petted each of the dogs who continued to peacefully sleep. "Mike, I don't know much about it either. You know Roxie, my right-hand waitress at Kelly's Koffee Shop. She has a neighbor who fell and broke her hip. Her doctor felt she needed to spend some time in a nursing home before she went back to her own home.

"Roxie visited her yesterday, and while she was there she got to talking to the director of the Cedar Bay Nursing Home. You know how Roxie likes to talk. Anyway, from what she said, it's the only nursing home in the county, and her neighbor felt very lucky she was able to get admitted.

The director and Roxie were talking about recent changes in the nursing home industry, and she told Roxie she'd just read an article in an industry journal about the positive effect dogs can have on patients during their period of recuperation. According to the article, it said after only five minutes with a dog, a patient's stress hormone, I think she said it was called 'cortisol,' went down substantially. I guess that would be pretty significant when people are recuperating and trying to regain their health."

"Well, that's probably true, but I fail to see what any of that has to do with you," Mike said.

"Here's the thing. Our dogs have been in the coffee shop a number of times, in fact Lady and Skyy were just puppies when I started taking them to work with me. Anyway, long story short, Roxie told her how well-trained and gentle Rebel was and suggested she call me to see if I'd be interested in visiting the nursing home with him, maybe once or twice a week. She called me, and I agreed to do it. Since I really don't have time to help out at the animal shelter, I felt this would be a way for me to give back to the community, and we're going the day after tomorrow. This is all new territory for me and for Rebel, so I'll just have to wait and see how it goes."

"Between keeping the coffee shop open all week and with all there is to do here at the house, to say nothing of when your children and grandchildren visit, I'm not really sure you need to take on anything new. Seems to me the nursing home and the patients have survived without you and Rebel so far, and they probably could continue to get along just fine."

Kelly started to interrupt him, but he stopped her and said, "Just a minute, I haven't finished what I was going to say. What I was getting ready to say is that I know if your mind's made up about something, that's it, and I'd be wasting my breath if I said anything else. Would I be right?"

"Yes, and I'm glad you finally realize it. Now bear with me, I'm going to change the subject. I'll make you a deal. If you clean up the dishes, I'll fix dinner. How does that sound?"

"You're on," he said as he took the ringing cell phone out of his shirt pocket and said, "I better take this. It's my deputy, Brandon."

Kelly walked into the kitchen and began taking things out of the refrigerator and pantry in preparation for dinner. A moment later Mike walked in. "Kelly, I think dinner's going to have to wait, and I need your help. Evidently there was a fire in a farmhouse on the west side of town. Looks like it might have been set to disguise a murder that took place there."

"Oh, no. I'm happy to help, Mike, but you usually don't ask for it. How come this time?"

He motioned to the dogs to get in their kennels and turned to her. "Looks like the person who was killed had a lot of dogs in the house. They got out in time, but the Cedar Bay Animal Shelter is just about at maximum capacity as it is right now. I told Brandon you'd help the director, Jenna Lee, transport some dogs there. I'll take my patrol car, and you can follow me in your minivan."

"Do you know who was killed?" she asked as they walked towards the door leading to the garage.

"No. Brandon sounded pretty frantic, and I heard a lot of barking in the background. I'm sure he'll have a lot more to tell me when we get there. Ready?"

"Yes, somehow dogs have really become a big part of my life. I sure never saw all of this happening when I got Rebel from the deceased drug agent's wife a few years ago."

CHAPTER TWO

Mike turned on his siren, and Kelly followed him as they raced to the old farmhouse on the west side of town. Ten minutes later they parked their cars behind a fire engine in front of a house which was obviously the one where the fire had taken place. Mike got out of his car and hurried into the house with Kelly following right behind him.

"Mike, glad you're here," Brandon said. "The woman who was murdered is Maggie Ryan. Funny thing, she was my teacher when I was in elementary school. That was over twenty years ago. She was a spinster then, and from the looks of it, she never did get married. I have a couple of guys from the department securing the house as a crime scene and doing the necessary DNA gathering and dusting for fingerprints. Follow me."

They walked down the hall and entered the bedroom where the body of Maggie Ryan was lying, apparently killed by a gunshot to her chest. Although the fire had been quickly put out by the firemen, the smell of smoke was thick in the house.

"Brandon, it doesn't look like there was a lot of fire damage to the house. Did someone see the flames and call 911?"

"No, that's the strange thing, Sheriff. A call came in about barking dogs, but there was no mention of a fire. Looks like the fire was probably set deliberately to cover up any evidence concerning the

4

murder of Miss Ryan." He noticed Kelly standing behind Mike and said, "Mrs. Reynolds, Jenna sure could use some help with the dogs. She should be back any minute from making the first run to the animal shelter. Any chance you can give her a hand?"

"Of course. I'll go outside and wait for her. I see the coroner's van pulling up, and I know both of you have things you need to do right now, so I'll get out of the way and help Jenna. Don't worry, Brandon, we'll make sure the dogs are all right."

Kelly walked outside as the grey van with the words "Cedar Bay Animal Shelter" written on it drove up to the fence gate. Jenna's assistant, a young college student, got out of the van and opened the gate for her. Fortunately, the owner of the property had built a double gate so the dogs couldn't inadvertently get out of the yard. Kelly waved to Jenna and walked over to the van.

"Kelly, I'm so happy to see you. Brandon called and said you could help me, and believe me, I could sure use some help. This is Sam," she said gesturing to the young man who was putting leashes on dogs and then loading them into the van. "He drove the van while I made telephone calls. I was able to get some additional volunteers to help at the shelter. I don't know if Brandon mentioned it to you, but we're almost maxed out in space there as it is."

"That's what I hear. Do you have enough dog beds for them?"

"I told the volunteers to call Dr. Simpson, the vet, and see if he had any extras. I also told them to call a couple of the stores in town and see if they would donate a few beds. Since it's early evening, I think most of them will still be open. I also called the pet store, and they're going to donate some food. Dr. Simpson is coming out to the shelter once we get all of the dogs there and check them out. I need to keep these dogs away from the ones that are already at the shelter, because I have no idea what their shot record status is. What a mess."

Kelly put her hand on the young woman's shoulder and said, "Don't worry. We'll find a way to make this work. Would you ask Sam to give me a hand? I can take about four dogs at a time in my minivan. After we've each made a couple more trips, we should be able to get all of them to the shelter. By then we'll have a better idea what we're dealing with."

"Sam, when you're finished loading the van, give Kelly a hand," Jenna said to the young man who was putting the dogs in the animal shelter van. "Thanks, Kelly, see you at the shelter."

Two hours later, volunteers had cordoned off an area of the shelter grounds for the rescued dogs. Additional volunteers had picked up food, dog beds, pet dishes, and other necessities. Since Dr. Simpson didn't have any idea whether or not the dogs had been vaccinated, he gave each of them a rabies shot and a titer test. When he received the results from the titer tests, he'd be able to determine which of them, if any, would need further vaccines. He told Jenna that all of the dogs appeared to be healthy with one exception. She was a German shepherd who had a tag on her collar indicating her name was Betsy. He said given the number of dogs, it was amazing only one appeared to be in poor health. Dr. Simpson put Betsy in his van and told them he was going to run some tests on her and let the shelter know what he found.

"Jenna, I think I've done about as much as I can do for now. I have to be at the coffee shop at 6:00 a.m. tomorrow morning, so I'm going to take off," Kelly said. "I'll call you tomorrow and see how you and the dogs are doing. I have to say I'm surprised you didn't know someone in Cedar Bay had that many dogs in their home. I also wonder if anyone ever reported it. Seems Mike told me once we couldn't have any more dogs because three was the limit for one household. Guess there's some county ordinance regarding it."

"You're absolutely right, and I agree it's strange in a small town like ours someone wouldn't have reported it. Just goes to show you never know what's going on behind closed doors, and in this case, literally."

"Isn't that the truth. Try and get some sleep tonight. Tomorrow is probably going to be pretty busy. If you'd like me to, I could post a flyer about adopting the dogs in the coffee shop or taking a foster dog in for a few days."

"I'd really appreciate it. I'll put together a flyer with some of their pictures on it and bring it in to you tomorrow. That might spark some interest. Kelly, thanks for all your help tonight. When I got to the house and saw how many dogs there were, I was completely overwhelmed."

"Happy to do it. See you tomorrow," Kelly said as she got in her minivan. She'd been so busy with the dogs she'd left her cell phone in the van. When she checked it for messages she saw there was a voicemail message from Mike.

"Hi, love. Sorry, but I won't be home tonight. The fire chief and his men are still looking at the arson angle, and Brandon and my men are searching the house for clues. When I finish up here, I need to go to the station and write up a report. By the way, you might know the woman who died. Her name was Maggie Ryan. Guess she was a retired teacher here in Cedar Bay. You might have even had her as a teacher. That's pretty much all I know. Sleep well, say good night to the dogs for me, and I'll see you tomorrow."

Mike was right, she thought. *I did have Miss Ryan for a teacher, but I haven't seen her for years. It was so long ago I don't remember much about her other than she was a spinster and had white hair she wore coiled up on top of her head. I think both of my kids even had her as a teacher. I vaguely remember going to a couple of teacher's conferences with her. Poor thing. No one deserves to die the way she did. I've got a personal interest in this murder. Might have to help Mike try and catch the killer even though he wouldn't think he needed my help, but he sure has been happy in the past when I've helped him.*

When Kelly got home from the shelter, Rebel, Lady, and Skyy sniffed every inch of her, wondering where and how she'd picked up so many different dog smells. "Guys, be happy you're here, and there are only three of you. You don't know how lucky you are." She fixed herself a sandwich, took a quick shower, got in bed, and quickly fell asleep.

CHAPTER THREE

"Shannon, what's goin' on over at the Ryan house? I was watchin' TV in the other room, and thought I heard sirens. See anything?" Ralph Lewis asked his wife who was standing to the side of the front room window peering out at the house across the street.

"Ralphie, you know as much as I do. There's a fire engine, a sheriff's car, and a minivan. I can also see a Cedar Bay Animal Shelter van. Looks like they're puttin' all them dogs ol' lady Ryan had in that van and the minivan. Good riddance, I say."

"Yeah, always did wonder how the old lady got away with havin' all them dogs in her house. Somethin' off with her. Seems like most everybody in Cedar Bay had her fer a teacher or their children did. Maybe that's why nobody said anything. Kind of weird livin' out your last days alone with a bunch of dogs, if you ask me."

Shannon continued to look out the window and said, "Well, I'll be darned. Looks like they're carryin' someone out of the house. It must be the ol' lady 'cuz I'm purty sure she was the only one that lived there. She must be dead 'cuz she's in what looks like a body bag, you know the kind ya' see on TV. Sorry anybody has to die, but I sure am tired of them dogs barkin' day and night. It's enough to drive me crazy. Wonder what she died from," she said idly, rubbing her fingers back and forth on the window curtain.

"Probably just old age. Have you been lookin' out the window fer long?"

"Nah, not that long. I heard the dogs' infernal barkin' jes' like usual, and when I looked out the window, there were dogs runnin' all over the place. That's when I seen the other cars. Well good, maybe now if they cart all them yappin' dogs away we can have a little peace and quiet. Didn't mind when she had a couple of dogs, but in the last year or so she just kept addin' to the group. Weird. Maybe the old lady jes' went nuts. You read in the paper almost every week about some old lady who dies and has a ton of cats, well maybe she just became a crazy dog lady instead," she said as she tightened her grip on the curtain.

"What do you see, Shannon? Somethin' else goin' on over there?" He stood behind her trying to see what was causing her to stare fixedly out the window.

"Ralphie, ya' know how they always have yellow tape around the scene of a crime in the movies and on TV? Well, guess what? Some guy wearin' a sheriff's uniform just put it all around the house. Maybe the old lady didn't die from, what do they call 'em, natural causes," she said excitedly.

"Shannon, if I didn't know better, I'd think you were enjoying this."

"Ralphie, how can you say that. Jes' thinkin' to myself that maybe it's some kinda justice. We've been talkin' fer months about them dogs, and if she was killed, maybe we weren't the only ones they bothered. I'm glad I won't have to see that hunch-backed ol' lady anymore. Jes' sayin', if ya' know what I mean."

"Well, sooner or later, I'll bet somebody will be comin' over here to interview us," Ralph said. "Make sure you don't say nuthin' about them dang dogs driving us nuts and how much we hated their barkin'. Last thing I want to do is draw any attention to us, not that we had anything to do with it anyway, right?"

"Right, Ralphie. As usual, yer' absolutely right," Shannon said with a slight smile playing at the sides of her mouth. She continued to look out the window while Ralph walked back into the den to watch TV.

CHAPTER FOUR

The next morning Kelly woke up before the alarm clock went off and reached over and turned it off. She wasn't sure what time Mike had come home in the early hours of morning, but she knew the last thing he needed was to be awakened prematurely by a ringing alarm clock. She let the dogs out in the back yard, made a pot of coffee, and got dressed for what she knew would be a busy day.

A few minutes later she let the dogs back in the house. They immediately returned to their dog beds in the room where Mike was peacefully sleeping. She walked into the garage and pressed the garage door opener, hoping the noise of it going up and down wouldn't wake him.

"Kelly, good morning. Think it'll be busy today?" Roxie asked as Kelly opened the door to Kelly's Koffee Shop. Before Kelly could answer, Charlie, the line cook who had been with her for years, and Molly, the relatively new waitress who had replaced Madison, walked into the coffee shop.

"Might as well tell all of you at the same time," Kelly said. "Maggie Ryan was murdered last night. She taught school a lot of years in this town, so she was pretty well known. Kelly's is always busy whenever there's some tidbit of gossip to talk about, and I'm sure we'll be filled with curious people from the time we open until we close."

"I didn't hear anything about it," Roxie said. "I had Miss Ryan, that's what we all called her, in sixth grade. She was a good teacher, but I haven't heard anything about her in years."

"Me, too," Charlie said. "All the kids on the reservation had her for a teacher as well. We had to be bussed into Cedar Bay to go to school, since we didn't have our own school. Matter of fact, I'll bet most of the people in Cedar Bay had her as their teacher. What happened?"

Kelly told them what she knew about the murder, the fire, and the dogs Maggie Ryan had on her property. "I think we need to quit talking and get to work. You each know what you need to do, so let's get started."

The first customer came through the door at 6:30 and, just as Kelly had predicted, from then on, the coffee shop was jammed with people who'd heard about the death of Maggie Ryan. The four of them worked as fast as they could and still could barely keep up with the orders.

At 11:30 that morning, Kelly looked up and saw Jenna from the animal shelter motioning to her. "Good morning, Jenna. Did you survive the night? How's everything out at the shelter? Let me see if I can find you a seat."

"To answer your question, it's a zoo. I have every volunteer on our roster out there, and they're calling their friends and asking them to give us a hand. As far as a seat, I can't stay. I just stopped by to drop off the flyer we talked about last night. I photographed some of the dogs I thought would be the most appealing and put pictures of them on it. I'm hoping people will come to see them and also want to adopt some of the others. Dr. Simpson is giving anyone who adopts one of the dogs a discount on spaying or neutering. In my eyes, that man's a saint, but then again I think everyone who's donated things to the shelter is too."

"I don't have any extra dog items, but if you'd like, I could take some food from the coffee shop out to the shelter after we close.

Would that help?"

"Absolutely, at this point we'll take all the freebies we can get. I have no idea how we're going to be able to keep the doors of the shelter open once these freebies stop. The food alone is a huge cost."

"Don't worry. I'm sure something good will come out of this. I think I'll make an announcement right now to everyone who's here, and then I'll tape the flyer to the front door, so people will see it when they come in."

Kelly stood up on a chair and clapped her hands to get the diners' attention. "Could I have your attention for a moment?" she asked. "Thanks," she said when the coffee shop became quiet. "This is Jenna Lee, the director of the Cedar Bay Animal Shelter," she said smiling down at Jenna. "By now I'm sure all of you have heard that Maggie Ryan was murdered in her home last night. What you may not know is that there were over thirty dogs on her property.

"The shelter has taken in the dogs for now, but they're stretched beyond their capacity, both in terms of space and money. If any of you could adopt one or two of the dogs, give a donation, or even act as a foster home until things get settled, it would really be appreciated. I'm taping a flyer to the front door of the coffee shop. Take a look and think about giving someone an early Christmas present or even give yourself one. Thanks for listening. Now you can get back to your food."

"Wait a minute Kelly," Roxie said. "I think we'd like to know if all of the dogs are healthy."

"I can answer that," Jenna said. "Dr. Simpson examined them and with the exception of one of them, Betsy, a German shepherd, they're all fine."

"What was wrong with that one?" Roxie asked.

"It looks like she may have been running loose on the streets for awhile. She had a lot of cuts on her and some dried blood. Dr.

Simpson thinks that Miss Ryan probably just got her, anyway, he took her to his clinic to run some tests on her and make sure she's going to be okay."

"Will she go back to the animal shelter when she's healed?"

"I imagine. We just haven't gotten that far. Is there some reason you're asking?" Jenna said.

"My son has always wanted a German shepherd. When you mentioned her, it seemed like some kind of sign from up above or something like that."

"Why don't you take your son to Dr. Simpson's and see what he thinks of Betsy?"

"I just might do that, but think I better talk to my husband first," Roxie said, laughing.

Kelly was still standing on the chair listening to the interchange between Roxie and Jenna when she heard a familiar voice say, "Let me help you down, Kelly," Doc, a friend and a lunchtime regular said. "I heard some rumors at the clinic this morning, and from what you just said, I guess they're true. I assume it's Mike's case. I don't think I ever met the lady."

"You probably didn't know her Doc, since you haven't lived here in Cedar Bay that long, and yes, Mike's in charge of the murder investigation. You better grab a seat at that booth over there. Today's a day when finding a place to sit is almost impossible. I can save you the time of looking at the menu, because I made pesto stuffed pork chops yesterday before all of this happened. They're fully cooked and just need to be heated. If you need a recommendation, when I served it to Mike last week he said it was one of the best things he'd ever eaten. I'd also recommend the two kinds of monkey bread Charlie made. One's an herb bread, and the other is sweet and sticky. It's made with brown sugar and pecans. If you're interested, I'll turn the order in for you."

"If Mike said that, and you recommend it, then it's good enough for me. I heard you say the director of the shelter was looking for foster homes. I've got a pretty big fenced yard and I think Lucky, the yellow Lab you gave me, would love to have one or two new friends. Think I'll go out to the shelter before my next appointment at the clinic."

"Doc, that would be great. I know Jenna would really appreciate it. Give me a call after you go there. I'd like to hear what happens. I'd love to stay and talk, but we're really swamped. See you later."

CHAPTER FIVE

Jimmy Richards opened the front door of his home and announced in a loud voice, "Amanda, I'm home. What did you fix me for lunch today? Is Allen here yet? I've got a bunch of boxes that need to be unloaded at the store, and yesterday he said he'd give me a hand. Find out anything of interest at the prayer meeting this morning?"

"In answer to your first question, I made a corned beef on rye sandwich and set out some chips and a pickle for you. For dessert, I made an apple cloufitis. That apple tree in our backyard is loaded with apples, so I used a bunch of them."

"What in the devil is a cloufitis? Sounds like some Frenchy thing."

She avoided his eyes and said, "It's kind of like a custard dish with apples. I think you'll like it. I got the recipe from that cooking channel I watch."

"I'll try it, but you know I'm not real big on Frenchy things. Say, why the blazes aren't you looking at me? What aren't you telling me?" he asked in a stern demanding voice as he sat down at the kitchen table and picked up his sandwich.

"Jimmy, Allen called a little while ago," she said hesitantly. "He's over in Portland with some friends. He remembered he'd told you he'd help you today. Said to tell you he'd do it when he got back in town." She walked over to the sink trying to ignore the furious look on his face.

"Swell, that's just swell," Jimmy said as he pounded his fist on the table. "Does he think those boxes will unload themselves, and where does he think the money comes from that lets him eat and sleep here, much less go to Portland? I tell you, it's all that stupid teacher's fault. He's never been the same ever since she tried to hold him back in school for a year. It seems like it somehow played with the thinking that goes on his mind. I'm sure she's the reason he started messing around with drugs. Come to think of it, that's probably what he's doing over in Portland right now.

"He told me once he felt like the laughingstock of the school when all of his classmates found out he'd be spending another year at the elementary school while they went on to junior high. I think that was the beginning of the end. We can't afford to send him to another drug rehab center. He's been to three of them already, and none of them have helped. Yep, it's all that teacher's fault. I'd like to dance on her grave," he said as he stuffed a handful of potato chips in his mouth.

"Jimmy, the third thing you asked me when you walked in the door was if I'd found out anything at the prayer meeting this morning. Well, the answer to your question is yes. I found out Maggie Ryan was murdered last night. She was the teacher you've been talking about."

Jimmy stopped chewing and said, "How did you find that out?"

"It was the main topic of conversation at the prayer meeting. I guess Reverend Barnes went out to her house a couple of times a week. He started doing that once her hunchback condition got so bad she couldn't drive to church anymore. The church secretary said Reverend Barnes was devastated because of her death. She said a lot of other people at the church had been students of Maggie Ryan's over the years, and even though she'd pretty much been a recluse for the last few years, a lot of her former students really loved her, even after all those years."

"Well, they may have, but that sure wasn't my impression of the old biddy. Way I see it, whoever killed her did mankind a real service. Yup, won't find me standing at her grave weeping. Maybe now that she's dead she'll have some time to think about how she messed up Allen's life."

"Jimmy, I'm not sure you can blame her for Allen's problems. Maybe they would have happened anyway."

"I do blame her, and I'm glad she's dead. Got what she deserved. Anyone say when she was murdered?"

"Yeah, early last night. Why?"

"Well, as you know, I had to work last night getting those boxes off the truck and into the warehouse. Don't think it'll come to this, but if anyone asks if I was home last night, just tell them yes."

"Jimmy, I can't lie. You didn't get home until around nine last night."

"Amanda, I said I was home last night, and I'd like you to repeat that," he said in a threatening tone of voice, as he glared at her with an evil look in his eyes.

Amanda, recognized the all too familiar look on his face and knew she had to comply with his demand or else she would pay a dear price for not obeying him. "Yes, Jimmy, you were home last night," she said in a timid voice as she turned away from him, unable to face him because of a growing sick feeling in her stomach.

CHAPTER SIX

"Thanks, Kelly, this looks delicious," Doc said as she placed a pork chop with mango coleslaw in front of him along with a plate containing two kinds of monkey bread.

"Doc, try a bite of that coleslaw. Today's the first day I've served it, and I really like it. I think it's more of a warm weather dish, but even though it's fall, I think today officially qualifies as warm."

"I like it. No, make that I really like it. Any chance you could give the recipe for it to Liz? This is something I'd like to have at home."

"No problem, but it's so easy I'm almost embarrassed to give it to you. I'll write it down, and you can take it with you when you leave. Doc, hate to ask this of you, but seeing how busy it is today, if you see somebody you know, I'd appreciate it if you'd share your booth. Thanks, and I'll talk to you before you leave." She hurried back to the service window separating the dining room from the kitchen and grabbed an order that was ready for a customer.

Doc spent the next few moments enjoying his meal. He was startled when he felt a hand on his shoulder. "Sorry to bother you, Doc," Reverend Barnes said, "but Kelley said you might be willing to share your booth with me and seein' how busy this place is, I'd really appreciate it. It's been a draining morning for me."

"Of course, Reverend, happy to do it. Sit down," he said gesturing to the seat on the other side of his booth. "By the way, if you're hungry, sure do recommend the pork chop, coleslaw, and monkey bread."

"Thanks. Even making a decision as to what I should have for lunch is almost too much for me at this point."

"Hi, Reverend. Ready to order?" Roxie asked.

"I'll take what Doc's having. Looks good. Thanks, Roxie."

"May take a little longer than usual. We're really jammed right now. Just want you to know up front, so you won't think I forgot to turn in your order."

"Not a problem, Roxie," the reverend said. "It'll get here when it gets here, and that's fine with me." She walked away to place his order, and he sat back in the booth, tiredly rubbing his eyes.

"Reverend, looks like you got the weight of the world on your shoulders today. Want to talk about it?" Doc asked.

"This is a difficult time for me," Reverend Barnes said. "One of my parishioners was murdered last night. I feel close to all of my parishioners, but I was particularly close to this one."

"I heard that a woman by the name of Maggie Ryan was murdered last night. Can't believe there'd be two murders on the same night in this small town, so I'm assuming that's the woman you're talking about. Would I be right?" Doc asked.

"Yes, I just can't believe anyone would want to murder Maggie. She not only taught school to most of the people living in this town, but she also was a strong believer in the way of the Lord. The other parishioners and I are devastated by her death. I visited her twice weekly, and we prayed together. It's just a tragedy," the reverend said.

"I hear she had a lot of dogs out at her place. The director of the

Cedar Bay Animal Shelter was here a little while ago, and Kelly made a plea on its behalf for people to adopt the dogs, donate whatever anyone could afford, or even foster a dog or two for a while. Thought I'd go over there after lunch and see if I can help," Doc said. "You said you prayed with her when you visited her. What in the world was she doing with all those dogs? I heard she had around thirty."

"She did. I know that's way over the limit set by the county, but she felt compelled to open her heart and her house to dogs. She found them at different shelters on the Internet, and people brought them to her. When I went over there, she let them out in the yard, so we could pray together without all the commotion they created."

"Since I only came to Cedar Bay a few years ago, it's not surprising that I never met her. Did she have any relatives?" Doc asked, taking the last bite of his pork chop.

"Not that I know of. She was a spinster, and after she retired from teaching, she pretty much became a recluse. Just her and those dogs. One time she mentioned something about a friend visiting her from time to time, but I don't know who that was."

"Sad thing when someone kills an old woman," Doc said. "Sure doesn't make sense to me. If she was a recluse, wonder how she got the food to feed all those dogs."

"She told me once she loved the Internet, because she could get whatever she needed for the dogs delivered to her home, and she didn't have to leave it. As for your question about relatives, I don't think she had any since she told me once she'd named me as the beneficiary of her estate, although I doubt she had very much in the way of an estate. She sure didn't live that way. She even gave me her will for safekeeping and told me to use the money for the good of the church. Guess I probably need to get it probated. I'll call Lem Bates this afternoon and make an appointment."

"What about a funeral? Is there going to be a big do at the church?"

"No. She told me on a number of occasions that if anything ever happened to her she wanted to be cremated and didn't want any type of a service to be held. She was afraid everybody she'd taught would feel they should pay their last respects to her, and the service would end up turning into a zoo. As religious as she was, she didn't want to be the reason something like that might happen. She may have been right. She was always thinking of other people. Maggie really was one of the finest people I've ever known."

"Sounds like it. I've got to go, Reverend. It's been nice talking to you, but if I want to get out to the shelter before my next appointment, I better leave now," Doc said as he got up from the booth, taking his check with him.

"I need to leave too. I've got things I need to do, and I'm sure this open booth is going to make someone happy."

Together, they walked over to where Molly was standing at the cash register. "Doc, here's the recipe you wanted. Kelly asked me to give it to you and apologize for not being able to talk to you a little more, but she said to tell you she's really busy today."

"Tell her thanks, and it wasn't a problem," Doc said as he followed the reverend out the door. The reverend looked at his watch and hurried to his car. Doc noticed something fall from the reverend's wallet as he was putting it in his back pocket. He stooped down and picked up the piece of paper. "Reverend," he called out, but Reverend Barnes was already in his car heading back to his church.

Doc looked down at the piece of paper and thought *Why would the reverend carry this in his wallet? That's strange.*

CHAPTER SEVEN

When Doc walked into the Cedar Bay Animal Shelter he said to the young woman who greeted him, "Hi, I'm Doc Burkhart. Heard you have a number of dogs that were brought in last night that need a foster home for a few days. Thought I'd see if I can help you out. Could you show me where to go?"

"Yes, that would be wonderful. My name's Sherri, and I'm a friend of someone who volunteers here. I told her I could help for a few hours, so I don't know much. The dogs that were brought in last night are back this way. They've been sectioned off from the other dogs for the time being." She led Doc out the door and over to the far side of the building where he was greeted by dogs of every breed and kind that were confined in a large fenced-in exercise area. All of them seemed to be barking and running around at the same time. They presented a scene that could only be described as mass pandemonium.

If I had to work here with all this commotion, I'd go crazy, he thought. *Glad there's people like Sherri in the world, because I'm one of those who would rather write a check and take a dog home to some peace and quiet.*

He spent the next twenty minutes walking along the fence looking at the dogs. When he spotted a bulldog puppy, he remembered he'd often thought they were cute, and how he'd always thought he'd get one someday. He let out a low whistle and to his surprise, the little bulldog ran over to the fence, sat, and started wagging the back end of his body. His stubby little tail was so short it could barely move. Drool ran out the side of his mouth and collected in a puddle next to his front feet. He became so excited he started running around in circles, unable to contain his excitement that someone had noticed him.

Okay, that's it, Doc thought. *I'll take him home with me tonight. Hopefully they can keep him until I can pick him up after the clinic closes for the day. I just hope this will be okay with Liz. Dogs are kind of a new thing for her, and while I know she loves Lucky, I'm not sure how she's going to feel about another dog in the house. Anyway, it's just for a few days. I'll tell her when I get back to the clinic. I remember she said she was jammed this afternoon seeing patients in her psychology practice.*

He stood up and walked over to where Sherri was talking on her phone. She turned to him when she ended the call and asked, "Find one you can foster for a few days?"

"Sure did. I'd like to foster that little bulldog puppy. Any chance I could leave him here for the rest of the afternoon and pick him up when I get off work? I'd be here around 6:15 this evening."

"Of course, and thank you so much. He'll be ready for you. Actually, even though I've only been here for a few hours, if I could take one of them home with me, he'd be the one. He's one of the friendliest dogs I've ever seen."

"I sure hope so," Doc said. "I've got a yellow Lab at home that hasn't been around other dogs all that much, and he's pretty spoiled. Hope the two of them can work it out."

"I didn't see the house where the dogs came from, but I'd think if the puppy could get along with thirty or so other dogs, he could get along with one," Sherri said. "I'll put a big note on his photo that he's going to be fostered this evening."

Doc took his wallet out of back pocket and said, "Happened to go to the bank this morning, so I have a little more cash with me than usual. Here's my contribution to the shelter. You're doing good work here. Keep it up and thanks." He handed her five $20 bills and walked out to his truck, leaving the astonished young woman looking after him.

When he got back to the medical clinic he and his wife, Liz, jointly operated, he walked into her reception room and said, "CeeCee, any chance I can talk to Liz before she gets tied up with patients?"

"Sure, Doc, she's reading a file getting ready for her first appointment of the afternoon. You have a couple of minutes."

He knocked lightly on the door to Liz's office and heard her say, "Come in." He opened the door and walked in.

"Hi, sweetheart," she said to her husband of nearly two years. "How was lunch? I would have joined you, but I got tied up with someone who was having a crisis. Unfortunately, that took precedence. How's Kelly?"

"She's fine. I don't know if you've heard, but there was a murder in town last night. A retired school teacher, guess she'd become almost a hermit, was murdered in her home. That was bad, but then it looks like whoever killed her set fire to the house, probably trying to cover up the murder. One of Mike's deputies got there in time to alert the fire department, and they were able to put out the fire without a lot of damage to the house. Interesting thing was the old lady had some thirty dogs in her house. They were all taken to the Cedar Bay Animal Shelter. Guess Kelly helped transport them there."

"Oh, that's terrible news. Do they have any idea who did it?"

"Not from what I heard. Guess the shelter is really overloaded with dogs. They were asking for volunteers to foster some of the dogs."

"Okay, Doc, I know you well enough to figure out there's more to this conversation than just keeping me up to date on the latest news in Cedar Bay. Anything you want to tell me?"

"You ever been around a bulldog?" he asked with a sheepish look on his face.

"Can't say that I have, but why do I have the feeling I'm probably going to be?"

"Well, with your permission, I told the shelter I'd like to help them out. See, there was this little bulldog puppy, and I've always been a sucker for that breed. I kind of told them I'd be back after work to pick him up and take him home for a couple of days. You know, just until they can get things under control. What do you think?" he said looking over at the far corner of the room so as to avoid making eye contact with her.

"Doc, Lucky is the first dog I've ever been around, and I wasn't sure how I'd feel about having a dog. Since we've been married, as you know, I've become completely devoted to him, so sure, let's take the bulldog in for a few days and see what happens. Feel better, now that you fessed up?" she asked grinning.

"Yeah, I sure do. I think the little guy will be fine with Lucky. I'm just not sure how Lucky is going to react to him. He's been pretty spoiled by us. Anyway, I told them I'd be there after the clinic closes this evening, around 6:15. Can you go with me or do you have a late appointment? If you do, I'll circle back and pick you up."

Liz looked at the calendar on her desk and said, "It looks like I can go with you, barring an emergency. My last appointment is at 5:00 this evening. I'm assuming since the dog's owner died, we don't have a name for him. Right?"

"Probably. Just looking at him, I don't think he could be more than two or three months old. Wonder how she got him, but we'll probably never know. Think about it, and we'll come up with a name on the way there. See you then," he said as he walked out of her office and closed the door behind him.

CHAPTER EIGHT

When Liz and Doc got to the shelter that evening, he walked over to the volunteer he'd met, Sherri, and said, "We're here to pick up that little bulldog I talked to you about earlier. What do I owe you?"

"Not a thing. Everyone's been so generous we're not charging anything for the people who are taking dogs to foster or even adopt right now. I'll have Sam get him for you."

A few minutes later a young man with a big smile on his face walked up to Doc and Liz with a squirming little bulldog puppy in his arms. "If I could have taken one home, he'd be my choice. There's just something about him, but my mom would kill me.

"We already have two dogs and a cat, and she's told me in no uncertain terms we aren't getting any more pets. I'm leaving for college in a few weeks, so I really can't get a dog now and abandon it almost immediately. Would you hold him while I get a dog bed for him? We had a big donation of them, and we're giving one to everybody who fosters one of the dogs," he said as he handed the puppy to Doc.

Liz clipped the leash they'd brought with them to the collar the shelter had put on the puppy, then Doc put him down and walked him over to a grassy area.

"Doc," Liz said walking with them, "I think he looks like a Max would look. How about that for his name?"

Doc looked down at the puppy who was busy communing with nature and said, "It fits him. He does look like a Max. That's his name from now on, or until we return him to the shelter," he said looking over at Liz.

She smiled and said, "I think that's a nonissue. I have a feeling not only are we a two-car family, we've just become a two-dog family. How do you think we should introduce him to Lucky?"

"Well, since the back yard at the ranch is fenced, I think we'll just let him out there and put Lucky there as well. Lucky's been around Kelly's dogs and was fine with them. I think it'll be okay, at least I sure hope so." He looked down at the puppy who was jumping on his leg and begging for attention. "Max, training starts now. Off. Off," he said firmly pushing the dog into a sitting position. "Sit, Max, sit." Even though he was wiggling, the little puppy sat looking up at Doc with adoring eyes. He'd found his person and didn't want to disappoint him.

Doc looked over at Liz and said, "Piece of cake. This one's going to be easy to train. I can feel it in my bones. Max, come," he said as he walked to his truck, the dog dutifully walking as fast as his stubby little legs would let him.

"I'm going to remind you of this moment in a few weeks after you've been up several times a night with him, cleaned up his accidents, and lamented about all your things that he's chewed up," Liz said laughing.

"Liz, I'm going to put the dog bed on your lap, so you can make sure he doesn't jump out and end up on the floor of the truck causing an accident." All the way home Max stayed in his dog bed and licked Liz's hand and face, showering her with doggie kisses.

When they got home, Doc turned the engine off, walked around to the passenger side, and took Max out of his dog bed. "Okay, Max, it's show time. This is when you get to meet Lucky. Break a leg."

Doc held Max in his arms and strode around to the side of the house. He opened the gate and set Max on the ground. When he walked away, Max started yipping, not wanting to be left alone. Liz went into the bedroom where they kept Lucky's kennel, opened it, and let him out into the back yard through the sliding glass door. Doc joined her as they watched the two dogs sniff and circle each other. Within minutes Lucky was lying on his back and Max was happily jumping on him. As they continued to play, Liz turned to Doc and said, "Think we're home safe, Doc. Looks like there's not going to be a problem."

"Thank heavens. I know I don't show many emotions, and my ex-wife would have been the first one to tell you that, but I've been a nervous wreck all afternoon about this."

"I know, Doc. That's what makes me a good psychologist and why our marriage works. You don't have to tell me or explain your emotions to me, because I pretty much know what's going on inside your head all the time."

He took her face in his hands and said, "Thank you for just being you. I never thought I would be happy again after that debacle in Southern California, and I owe it all to you."

"You are more than welcome, but I think you have to give a lot of the credit to Kelly. She's the one who believed in you and cleared your name. Actually, she's the one who knew before you did that you'd be right for me, so I guess we both owe her a big thank you."

"And," Doc said pulling away from her, "She's also the one who gave me Lucky and is kind of responsible for that little bundle of energy we just brought home. Speaking of which, I need to go out in the garage. I had a small wire kennel for Lucky when he was a puppy, and I put it up in the rafters. Might as well get Max kennel trained sooner rather than later. I'll be back in a few minutes. Just leave them outside until I get back."

*****

After dinner was over and the dogs were asleep on their beds, Doc remembered the piece of paper that the reverend had dropped on the ground after lunch. For some reason, it bothered Doc, and he decided to go into his office and take a look at the website that was written on the paper.

He typed the URL address in and looked at the graphic that appeared on the screen. Certain he'd made a mistake, he retyped the address and the same graphic come up again.

Why would the reverend have this website written on a piece of paper in his wallet? He's the last person in the world I'd think would be looking at an online gambling site. That makes absolutely no sense at all.

While he was trying to figure out what the connection could be, his cell phone rang. "Doc, it's Kelly. I went over to the shelter after work and took a bunch of food. Figured all those volunteers could use some. I had a lot of frozen cookie dough in the freezer and when it slowed down a little after lunch, the staff and I baked cookies and bagged them for the volunteers. I think they appreciated it, but that's not why I'm calling. I hear you have a new addition to the family. Any truth to that?"

"Yeah, the truth is asleep in his dog bed in the other room as we speak. We named him Max. He and Lucky seem to get along fine, so he's got a home for a few days."

"Doc, knowing you, I imagine Max has found a permanent home, and he couldn't ask for a better one. How's Liz handling the situation?"

"She likes him. Max really is adorable. He sat on her lap in his dog bed all the way home and spent the whole time giving her doggie kisses. Think that might have sealed the deal in Liz's eyes. By the way, Kelly, how well do you know Reverend Barnes?"

"Not well. When I attend church, I go to the Catholic Church, so

I'm very familiar with Father Brown, but I only know Reverend Barnes from when he's been at the coffee shop for lunch. Other than that, I don't know much about him. I saw him sitting at lunch with you today. Why do you ask?"

"We left the coffee shop together after we'd paid for lunch. He was a little ahead of me and dropped a piece of paper on the ground that fell out of his wallet. Evidently he was in a hurry, because even though I called out his name, he got in his car and left before I could return it to him. Apparently he didn't hear me."

"And?"

"Here's the and. I picked the piece of paper up and stuffed it in my pocket. A few minutes ago, I remembered I had it. I took it out of my pocket, and it had a website written on it. I just pulled it up on my computer, but I don't know what to make of the website that came up."

"What was the website?" Kelly asked.

"It was an online gambling site. Somehow I'm having trouble thinking that the reverend is looking at online gambling sites. That's why I asked you how well you know him. It seems very odd."

"I agree, but maybe one of his parishioners has a gambling problem and gave him that site's link. There could be a very logical reason why he wrote it down."

"Kelly, I just remembered something else. He told me at lunch he was very close to the woman who was murdered. Evidently he went to her house a couple of times a week to pray with her, because she was housebound. He said she'd made him the beneficiary of her will. The whole thing seems odd to me."

"Does to me, too, Doc. I'll tell Mike about it. Maybe he found out something today. I expect him home any minute. I won't keep you, but I sure was curious what Liz thought about the new addition. Glad it's working out."

"Me too, Kelly, more than you know. See you at lunch tomorrow."

CHAPTER NINE

When Reverend Barnes returned to his church office after lunch he spent some time sitting in front of his computer looking at different websites. Using a piece of paper, he wrote down the numbers shown on the spreadsheets displayed on the websites and then added up the numbers. He stared at the total amount for a moment, and shook his head in amazement.

I had no idea I owed that much. This is a disaster. I don't know how much is in Maggie's estate, but I can sure use it. I better call Lem Bates and get the probate of her estate started. I need that money, and I need it now. He picked up his phone and placed a call to Lem Bates, the sole attorney in the small town of Cedar Bay.

A moment later a female voice said, "This is the law office of Lem Bates. May I help you?"

"Yes," Reverend Barnes said, "I need to make an appointment with Mr. Bates. If he has time tomorrow to see me, that would be fine."

"May I ask what this is regarding?" she asked.

"Yes. I'm the beneficiary of the estate that belonged to a woman who was murdered yesterday evening, Maggie Ryan."

"Yes, I heard about that. It's hard to believe that something like

33

that could happen in a sleepy little town like Cedar Bay. If you'll hold, I'll check his calendar and see if he can fit you in tomorrow." The line was quiet for a moment, and then she said, "He could see you at 1:00 in the afternoon. Will that work for you?"

"Yes. I'll be there at 1:00. Thank you," he said ending the call.

I wonder how long it will take to get the money transferred to my account. I don't remember Maggie ever saying she had any relatives, so I don't think anyone will contest her will. I really need that money. I don't know how much longer I can hold off those awful collection agency people that keep making threatening phone calls to me. I owe a lot more money than I ever realized. He looked back at his computer and shook his head. *Maybe instead of paying them back, I should just bet the money I'm going to get from her. My luck's due to change,* he thought smiling, *so why not?*

*****

"Good afternoon, Lem. How was court?" his secretary asked as he opened the door to his law office.

"The same as always. It's the good guys versus the bad guys. Sometimes they win, sometimes we win," he countered walking over to her desk and setting down his briefcase. "Anything happen this afternoon I should know about?"

"Not much. I did get a call from a man who identified himself as a Reverend Barnes. I made an appointment for him to see you tomorrow at 1:00. Evidently he's the beneficiary of Maggie Ryan's estate."

"Really? Is that what he told you?" Lem asked with a raised eyebrow. "That's not quite how I remember she willed her estate, but it's been several months since we went out to her house, and she signed her will. I put it in my safe deposit box at the bank after she signed it and you and I served as witnesses." He looked at his watch. "It's a few minutes after five, and the bank's closed now, but I better get it first thing in the morning, particularly if my memory serves me right. Why don't you go ahead and leave now? I'm only going to be here a couple more minutes. See you in the morning."

He walked into his office and stopped in front of the file cabinet where he kept his files, pulled a drawer open, and leafed through the files which were in alphabetical order. When he got to the R's, he carefully looked at each one, finally coming to the file that was labeled Ryan, Maggie. He pulled it out, walked over to his desk, and sat down. For the next few moments he studied the notes he'd made after he'd been to her house the first time. He also noted he'd returned to her home a week later with his secretary, and Maggie's will had been properly executed by her, and witnessed by them. He'd made a note with the date he'd put it in his safe deposit box at the bank.

Lem looked out his window at the darkening sky and thought, *I think I better call Mike about this when I get home. I have a bad feeling about it.*

He turned off the light in his office, walked into the reception area, took his coat from the coat rack, and locked the door behind him on his way out. *Tomorrow is going to be an interesting day*, he thought to himself.

CHAPTER TEN

Later that evening, Rebel, Lady, and Skyy all rushed to the door leading to the garage, tails wagging in anticipation. Mike opened the door and said, "Hi everybody, I'm home. Kelly, where are you? You're the only one not standing at the door with your tail wagging."

"I'm in the kitchen fixing dinner, and even if you can't see it, my tail is definitely wagging," she said laughing.

A moment later the big burly sheriff walked up behind her and kissed the back of her neck. "That's what I like to hear. By the way, Kelly, I don't know how you do it, but you just get more beautiful with time." He put his hands on her shoulders and turned her around, breathing in her scent and looking at her green eyes, her porcelain-like complexion, and dark hair which was swept up in a bun, the silver and turquoise hair picks she always wore keeping it in place.

"Keep talking like that, Sheriff, and I just might allow you to join me for dinner. Go change your clothes, and I'll open a bottle of wine. I have one chilling, since I figured you probably had a rough day," she said pushing him away.

"There's no way to have a nice day when you're trying to solve a murder," he grumbled as he walked down the hall followed by three dogs looking for a treat or at the least, a pat on the head. "Back in a few."

Kelly opened the wine and poured two glasses. She took the small slider buns out of their package and set them, along with the frozen tuna patties, on a tray on the counter. She'd made the mango coleslaw and wasabi spread earlier as well as a tomato and avocado salad.

When Mike walked back into the kitchen she handed him a glass of wine and said, "We're in no hurry. Let me know when you're ready for me to start, and I'll have dinner on the table in about five minutes. She sat down across the kitchen table from him. "I'm really curious what you found out today. Solve Maggie's murder?"

"Not even close, sweetheart. It's really a difficult case. There are no witnesses, nothing turned up in the way of fingerprints, and although I put a priority rush on the DNA test, it too, was a big fat zero," he said taking a sip of wine.

"What about the arson angle? Did the fire chief find out anything?"

"He confirmed that the fire was deliberately set. His men found traces of gasoline on some rags that had been strategically placed in locations leading into Maggie's bedroom. Another thing that led him to believe it was arson is all the windows in the house had been opened as wide as possible. You may remember that an increase of oxygen is needed to make a fire really burn hot and fast, and the open windows provided that."

"Couldn't Maggie have been the one who opened the windows?" Kelly asked.

"Sure, but think about it. She was a spinster, and usually, in fact, almost always, when a woman lives alone safety becomes a priority, and I find it very difficult to believe an elderly woman would open all the windows in her house on a fall evening. That doesn't make a lot of sense to me."

"Well, Mike, she had over thirty dogs in the house with her. I'd think that would provide her with some level of comfort concerning her security."

"That's a good point, Kelly, and one I've thought about," he said as he rubbed his fingers on the stem of his wine glass, "but I still think someone deliberately set that fire. Even if she was the one who opened the windows, that doesn't explain the presence of gasoline and rags."

"That's true. I guess I'm struggling with why anyone would kill an elderly spinster. Did you have a chance to talk to any of the neighbors, although the houses on that street are set pretty far apart from each other."

"Yes, we canvassed the neighborhood, and no one saw anything. There was one neighbor I'm a little suspicious of, but I don't think it means anything other than I have a suspicious mind. I guess that's what comes from being a sheriff."

"What caused your antenna to go up with that neighbor?" Kelly asked as she stood up and walked over to the stove. "Okay with you if I start dinner? We can continue to talk while I cook."

"Sure. What's for dinner tonight?"

"Tuna sliders with mango slaw and wasabi sauce are the main show. I picked the last of our tomatoes this afternoon, so we're having a salad with those and avocado slices. For dessert, I made a kind of trifle-like dessert in those crystal glasses I inherited from Mom. I think you'll like it, because it has all your favorites like chocolate, raspberries, sponge cake and whipped cream in layers. I made them when I got home and put them in the refrigerator to chill. It turned out even better than I'd hoped. I might make them at the coffee shop. I always try to be a little creative and develop new recipes. You're my sounding board."

"Trust me, you're always creative, my love," he said grinning at her. "Back to your question as to why my antenna went up. There's a couple who live across the street and up about half a block, and Maggie's house is certainly within their line of sight. The husband seemed okay, but his wife's the one who kind of interests me."

"In what way?"

"Well, when I asked her if she'd seen anything recently that was suspicious, her answer was, 'What could possibly be suspicious about that old hunch-backed biddy? The only thing suspicious about her was why she had so many dogs, and why she let them bark all the time. Good riddance, if you ask me.' Seemed a little harsh to say something like that about a person who'd recently been murdered."

"I'll say. How do you intend to follow up on that?"

"I'm going to ask some of the other neighbors if there was any bad blood between the two women. It's pretty flimsy, but for now that's all I've got."

"Mike, a thought just occurred to me. Do you know Sunny Jacobs?"

"No, should I?"

"I've lived my whole life in Cedar Bay, and I pretty much know everyone. Sunny's the principal of the Cedar Bay Elementary School where Maggie taught. I've known her forever, and I consider her to be a friend, although I don't see her much. Occasionally she comes into the coffee shop, orders her usual Cobb salad, and we catch up. Rebel and I are going to visit the nursing home after work tomorrow, and since the school's only a block from there, I could stop by and see if she can tell me anything about Maggie. Would that be okay with you?" she asked as she poured him another glass of wine.

He looked at her and said, "It's okay only if you tell me everything she says, and you don't try to get involved in this case. I want to be very clear about this, because we've had some problems regarding this issue in the past. You are not to get involved in this case, do you understand?"

"No problem, Mike," she said as she sat down. "I'll tell you everything she says, under one condition."

"And the condition being?"

"You do the dishes tonight."

"I can certainly meet that condition, and I'm glad we're on the same page with this."

"Good. By the way, I've got some interesting news to tell you. Doc went to the animal shelter after lunch today, and he and Liz are fostering a bulldog puppy that came from Maggie's house, but I'll bet that dog never sees the shelter again. Anyway, does anybody know why Maggie had so many dogs? I wonder what caused her to keep so many dogs."

"Kelly, all of us have idiosyncrasies of one kind or another. I imagine people would be shocked that someone who looks like you do and appears to have it all together keeps a supply of bacon chocolate chip cookies in her minivan for emergency snacks. That probably wouldn't be considered normal behavior by a lot of people."

"Their loss. They don't know what they're missing," she answered. "You're probably the only person I know who doesn't have some sort of idiosyncrasy."

"Of course I do. I'm as normal as anyone else."

"I'll bite. Fess up."

He sat back in his chair and swallowed the last of his wine. "No matter what I'm going to be doing on any particular day, I have to read the newspaper comic strips before I leave the house. As soon as you go to work in the morning, I get my cup of coffee, sit down, and read them. And another idiosyncrasy is that I'm ready for dinner."

"Okay, like I said, it'll be ready in about five minutes, but I have a question. How can such an intelligent man like you feel compelled to read the comic strips every day?" she asked, shaking her head in disbelief.

"I'll make it even worse. I have to do that, or I know I'll have a bad day. There, I've said it. Guess we all have our oddities."

While they were eating dinner, Kelly said, "I forget to tell you what else Doc told me. It has to do with the Ryan case."

"Good grief, woman. Haven't we been married long enough for you to know that anything relating to one of my cases takes precedence over other topics?"

"I know, Mike, it's just that one thing kind of led to another. This is about Reverend Barnes. I'm sure you've met him, although the only times you've ever gone to church have been pretty much at my insistence, and we've always gone to the Catholic Church."

"Kelly, back to the point. What did Doc tell you?"

She told him about how Doc had shared his booth at lunch with Reverend Barnes, and he'd told Doc that Maggie had willed her estate to him. She went on to tell Mike about the piece of paper that had fallen out of the reverend's wallet and Doc had picked up. She concluded by telling him Doc had visited the website that was written on the piece of paper, and it was a site for online gambling. "Mike, why do you think the reverend had a piece of paper in his wallet with a gambling website URL written on it?"

Mike was quiet for several moments and then said, "Kelly, I have no idea. Maybe a parishioner gave it to him, or maybe he likes to gamble and look at gambling websites. Maybe that's his idiosyncrasy."

"I don't know. Somehow it doesn't seem normal for a reverend to be looking at gambling websites."

"Kelly, that's unlike you. By nature, you're not a very judgmental person. So what if he looks at gambling sites?"

"Intellectually, I know you're right. Emotionally, even though there isn't a commandment against it, actually the ten commandments were way before the web..."

Mike interrupted her. "Kelly, you're rambling."

"Okay, I can't give you a solid reason why it isn't right, but I just know in my heart of hearts, it isn't, so there."

"Fair enough. Should we call that another idiosyncrasy?" he asked, laughing and getting up from the table. "Go, the kitchen is now my domain, and the dishes await their wash and rinse."

CHAPTER ELEVEN

"I'll be back in a minute, Kelly. I just got a call I need to take," Mike said walking away from where he and Kelly had been watching television, the three dogs asleep at their feet.

"Hi, Lem. Your name came up on my cell phone screen, so I knew it was you. How are you? It's been awhile since we've talked."

"Well, considering what each of us does for a living, that's probably not a bad thing," Lem said, laughing. "A little situation has come up I need to run by you and see what your thoughts are."

"I'm all ears, Counselor, shoot."

He listened while Lem told him about the phone call his secretary had received from Reverend Barnes that afternoon, and how the reverend was under the impression he was to inherit Maggie Ryan's estate. He continued, "I was Maggie's attorney and was out at her house a few months ago for the purpose of revising her will. I couldn't remember exactly who she'd named as her beneficiary in the new will, but I didn't think it was the reverend. I decided to go to the bank tomorrow and get the will out of my safety deposit box after I was finished in court.

"Mike, I left my office about 5:15 or so this evening. When I was walking to my car I noticed that the lights were still on in the bank. I saw the manager, Gene, in there and knocked on the door. He asked if I wanted something, and I said I needed to get into my safe deposit box. I told him I was planning on doing it first thing in the morning, but if I could do it now it would be a lot easier for me, since I have to be in court tomorrow morning."

"I'm surprised he'd let you in," Mike said. "I've always found banks to be very rigid when it comes to enforcing their rules."

"That's true, but I grew up with Gene. We played baseball together in high school and even roomed together in college, so I wasn't too surprised he let me in. Anyway, that's not what I want to talk to you about.

"As I told you earlier, my secretary made an appointment with Reverend Barnes for 1:00 tomorrow afternoon. The purpose of the appointment, according to him, was to begin the process for probating Maggie Ryan's estate of which he's the sole beneficiary, or at least believes he is."

"I take it from the way you're saying this, that he's not. Would I be right, Lem?"

"Yes, here's the really interesting part. I took the will out of my safe deposit box and quickly left the bank. I didn't want anyone to see me in there after hours, because I figured it wouldn't look good for anyone to know that Gene had let me in after hours. It's also probably in violation of the bank's operational rules imposed by the State Banking Commission. Anyway, I came home, and before I even ate dinner I read the will."

"And?" Mike asked.

"It puts an interesting spin on your murder case," Lem said. "Maggie left her entire estate to the Cedar Bay Animal Shelter, and the reverend is not mentioned in the will. It's a habit of mine to keep a client's former will, so if there's ever a problem, I have it as well. The reverend was correct in that Maggie left everything in an earlier will to him, but what he doesn't know is that she drew up a new will, and based on what he told my secretary, I don't think he knows he's no longer the sole beneficiary of her estate."

Mike whistled and was quiet for a few moments. "Lem, I really appreciate you calling me with this information. This is the first solid lead I've had in the case. Are you going to keep the appointment with him tomorrow?"

"I'm planning on it. I believe he was acting in good faith when he made it. I think I owe it to him to tell him in person, and since the will is going to be filed with the court for probate, I won't be disclosing any confidential information. As soon as it's filed, it will be a matter of public record."

"Lem, I seem to remember several years ago you had to tell Jeff Black's wife she'd been cut out of her husband's will, and you asked me to sit in on your meeting with her. Would you like me to be there tomorrow for your appointment with Reverend Barnes?"

"I thought about it, Mike, but I don't think it's necessary. I've actually attended the reverend's church several times, so I don't anticipate any problems. If I change my mind, I'll let you know."

"Okay, your call, but I'd be happy to do it. Why don't you have your secretary sit in on the appointment? You could tell him something like that's what you always do when it involves wills and estates. Having a third party present might help keep his emotions in check. Thanks for calling. I really appreciate it, and if you have a little time after you meet with him, I'd like to know how it went."

"Consider it done. Have a good rest of the evening," Lem said as he ended the call.

Mike sat at the kitchen table for a few minutes digesting what Lem had told him and putting it together with what Doc had told Kelly about the gambling website.

Maybe it's more than an idiosyncrasy on the reverend's part. Maybe he's got a gambling addiction, is in debt, and murdered Maggie Ryan, as strange as that would be. Much as I hate to involve Kelly, she's worked on enough of my cases she might have some insights that could be helpful.

He walked into the great room, picked up the remote control, and turned the television off. "Kelly, it kills me to do this, but I'd like to get your input on something."

"Flattery will get you anywhere, Sheriff. What input would you like?"

He told her about Lem's phone call and his suspicions based on the call and what Doc had told her. "Kelly, what do you think?"

"Mike, I don't know what to think. I've met Reverend Barnes a few times, but I can't say I feel like I really know him. I know how you hate coincidences, and he certainly would have a motive if he does owe some money to online gambling sites, and having an elderly parishioner die who just happened to have named him in her will as her sole beneficiary doesn't sound all that good. I know you've told me to stay out of this, but I've become friends with the woman who's the secretary at the reverend's church. Mary comes into the coffee shop almost every day for lunch. I'll talk to her tomorrow, and see if I can find out anything."

"Okay, Kelly. Two things and two things only. You can talk to the secretary and the principal, and I'm okaying these just because you know the people, and you probably could find out more than I could." He glanced at his watch and said, "It's later than I thought, and we both need our sleep. I didn't get much last night, and you have to get up early. I'll let the dogs out."

"Wait one more minute, Mike. You said Lem told you that the Cedar Bay Animal Shelter was the beneficiary of Maggie's estate. I hear they're struggling financially. Being the recipient of an inheritance might just make them healthy. It certainly could be thought of as a motive."

"I suppose you're right. I better go out there and see the director. I'll tell her the terms of Maggie's will, but first I need to call Lem in the morning and ask him if it's okay for me to do that. Since the will's going to be made public sometime in the next few days, it shouldn't be a problem. Actually, it makes perfect sense that Maggie would give her estate to the shelter based on the number of dogs she had. She probably knew if anything happened to her the dogs would go to the shelter, and she decided to give her money to it so her dogs would be properly cared for. Kind of a new twist to the theme of little old ladies giving their estates to their cat or dog."

"This is starting to get very interesting, and as Scarlett O'Hara said, 'Tomorrow is another day,' at least I think she's the one who said it."

"She did," Mike said. "I saw a rerun of Gone with the Wind the other night, but once again I didn't like the ending. She and Rhett should have ended up together."

"Agreed," Kelly said walking down the hall.

CHAPTER TWELVE

Kelly's Koffee Shop was standing room only the following morning. The early birds began arriving a half hour before the posted opening time of 7:00 a.m. If anything, it was busier than the day before, because the people who hadn't found out until late yesterday about Maggie Ryan's murder hurried to Kelly's to find out if there was any news about who might be the murderer. The people who had been there the day before returned for the same reason. Almost everyone who came to Kelly's that morning had been a student of Maggie Ryan's.

Roxie walked by Kelly and whispered, "My husband, son, and I went to see Betsy at Dr. Simpson's. Poor thing is pretty torn up. Dr. Simpson thinks she's going to be okay, but he took a lot of X-rays yesterday, and didn't like the looks of some of them, so he's taking more this morning. He said he'd call me as soon as he knows anything. Unless there's something really wrong with Betsy, we're going to take her."

"That's wonderful. I know Betsy will have a good home, and you'll finally get a dog. You've been telling me for a long time how much you wanted one. This is great."

"I sure hope so. The way she looked, something could really be wrong with her. I'm trying not to get my hopes up, but I can't help it."

"I have a good feeling about it, Roxie. Let me know when you hear from Dr. Simpson." She turned to Molly and said, "I'd like to talk to Sunny Jacobs if she comes in for lunch today. You know her, don't you?"

"Of course. Fortunately, I never had to go to the principal's office for a private meeting with her, but sure, everyone who's gone to school in Cedar Bay for the last probably twenty or thirty years knows her. I think she remembers me, at least she waves to me every time she comes in here. I'll let you know if she comes in today, although with this crowd, it would be easy to miss someone."

"Thanks, Molly. It isn't unusual for everyone to gather here whenever there's something big going on in our little town. You just haven't worked here long enough to experience it. Everyone wants to find out about the latest rumor, and human nature being what it is, people don't want to miss any of the details when a murder takes place. And speaking of murder, it's unfortunate that we've had too many of them for a town this small."

Just then a couple walked up to the cash register to pay their bill. As Molly collected the amount due, Kelly hurried to serve the latest order Charlie had cooked. A few hours later she happened to look up and saw Molly waving to her. Standing next to her was Sunny Jacobs. Kelly walked over to where Sunny was standing near the entrance, looking around the crowded coffee shop for an open seat.

"Sunny, I was hoping you'd come in today. I'd really like to talk to you. Since there's nowhere to sit out here, why don't you join me in the storeroom? Can I have Charlie prepare your usual Cobb salad, and you can eat it while we talk? There's a small table back there where we can sit."

"Thanks, Kelly. That would be great, since I'm kind of tight on time. I insist that my teachers not be late to their classes, so I don't want to be one of those 'do as I say, not as I do' school principals."

"Follow me and I'll give your order to Charlie. I'll tell him to make it a priority. There are perks to being the boss," Kelly said laughing.

She turned towards Molly and said, "I'll be in the storeroom for a little while. Why don't you tell Roxie you'll be covering for me? Thanks."

"Kelly, I appreciate you doing this. I really do like to set an example, and I knew when I walked in the coffee shop and couldn't find a seat, I'd never make it back in time if I had to go somewhere else for lunch. So, what did you want to talk to me about?" Sunny said smiling up at Charlie as he placed the large salad along with an iced tea on the small table.

"I'm sure you're well aware that one of the retired teachers from the Cedar Bay Elementary School, Maggie Ryan, was murdered night before last."

"Of course. That was the primary topic of conversation at school yesterday."

"Sunny, you know my husband is the county sheriff, and this case falls within his jurisdiction. He didn't grow up in Cedar Bay, so he never met Miss Ryan. I've helped him with a couple of his cases in the past, and I thought since I know you, and Miss Ryan taught under you for a number of years, that you might be able to help. I guess what I'm asking is if you know if she had any enemies or if there was anything involving her that might help Mike solve the mystery of her murder."

Sunny was quiet for several long moments while she ate her salad, then she put her fork down and said, "Kelly, I've been struggling with this ever since I heard she was murdered. There was an incident several years ago, a rather nasty incident, but I can't believe it would have any bearing on the case, so that's why I'm reluctant to bring it up. Sometimes it's best to leave the past where it is."

"Normally I'd agree with you, Sunny, but this is a particularly strange case. You may have heard Maggie had over thirty dogs living in her house which is pretty unusual. I've also heard she'd become somewhat of a hermit the last few years. I'd really appreciate anything you could tell me. Right now, Mike has nothing to go on."

Although Sunny was quietly eating, Kelly sensed she was going through some inner struggle, a struggle over whether or not to tell Kelly about something she knew that might possibly be related to the death of Maggie Ryan. Finally, she said, "Kelly, I've decided to tell you about the incident involving Maggie Ryan, but I'd prefer it if you didn't tell anyone I was the one who told you. It may have nothing to do with the case, but at the time it was quite unsettling. Here's what happened.

"I think it was about ten years or so ago. I know it was very close to the time Maggie retired. Anyway, you know she taught sixth grade. She had a student she didn't feel she could in good faith allow to graduate from elementary school and continue on to junior high school."

"Why was that?" Kelly interrupted.

"From everything Maggie told me, the young man, actually a boy at that time, was having learning problems as well as emotional problems. He didn't seem to be as far along in his studies as his fellow classmates. Maggie felt it would be a disservice to him for her to allow him to move on to junior high school. She'd carefully documented all of the reasons for her decision and told me before she told the boy and his parents. I looked over her documentation and agreed with her. It was a very difficult decision, but Maggie was a very conscientious teacher."

"How did the boy and his parents take it?"

"Not well at all, particularly the father. It was as if his son's learning issues were a slap in his face. Maggie had asked the three of them to attend a parent-teacher conference, and she asked me to attend as well. I think she knew there were going to be problems, and there were. The father threatened to sue the school district, and he threatened Maggie with physical harm. If I remember right, I think he said something like 'If you don't let Allen graduate, I'll make sure you'll regret it until your dying day.'"

"He said that that during the meeting?"

"Yes," Sunny said. "He actually became quite enraged. He started pacing back and forth and shouting at us. When they left the meeting, he yelled that his attorney would be in touch with us."

"You said his parents attended the meeting," Kelly said. "How did the boy's mother take the news?"

"I've thought about that many times over the years, and I think she knew her son wasn't ready for junior high school. And something else, although I have nothing solid to base this on, and again, you did not hear this from me, but as an educator, I've attended a number of workshops dealing with domestic abuse, both physical and emotional. If I was ever going to make an assumption that someone was a victim of domestic abuse, it would be Mrs. Richards. She never looked at her husband during the entire meeting, and when they left she had a terrified look on her face. I hope I'm not reading more into it than was actually there, but if I were a betting person, I'd bet she was frightened her husband was going to take his anger out on her."

"What happened to the boy after that?" Kelly asked.

"His father transferred him to the junior high school in the Ocean Beach School District which is just a few miles up the coast. I heard he barely made it through junior high, and then he evidently dropped out of high school. There's something else, although this is strictly rumor. I heard he'd gotten into drugs, and his parents had put him in several rehabilitation facilities, but they didn't help him."

"Did his father follow through and sue the school district?"

"No, thank heavens. I've often thought he probably went to an attorney, and the attorney told him he didn't have a case."

"Just a couple more questions, Sunny, and then I know you have to leave. Did you stay in touch with Maggie Ryan after she retired?"

"I was in contact with her only once. I called her to say hello and see if the boy or his family had ever gotten in touch with her."

"What did she say?"

"She told me she never heard from them again after the parent-teacher conference I'd attended. They pulled their son out of school, and that was the end of it. She told me she was glad it hadn't gotten messy, because there was something about the man that frightened her."

"Sunny, I'm putting two and two together and wonder if I'm adding it up to four correctly. You said she retired not long after that incident. When she was teaching at your school were you aware of her interest in dogs?"

"No, and that's an interesting question, because I remember her saying something once in the teachers' lounge about not understanding why people would ever have more than one pet, because they required so much of a person's time and money."

"Just a couple more questions, I promise, Sunny. When you talked to her after she'd retired, did you have a sense that something was off with her? I mean, I find it strange that she'd say something like not having more than one household pet and then she winds up having over thirty dogs. Something doesn't ring true."

"No, when I talked to her she seemed pretty much like she'd always been. She told me she spent a lot of time reading and that she had developed a bad case of osteoporosis, so she spent almost all of her time at home."

"Was she close to any of the other teachers?"

"Yes, I believe she and Linda Devine were close to each other. Their rooms at the school were side-by-side, and I remember once or twice hearing her mention that she'd visited Maggie and her osteoporosis was getting worse and worse, almost causing her to be bent over double. Rather ironic that I heard that Linda recently fell down the stairs in her home and broke her hip. Evidently she's convalescing at the nursing home we have here in town.

"Kelly, I really do need to leave. Thanks for allowing me to have lunch back here and please thank Charlie for me. The Cobb salad was excellent, as always." She stood up and started walking toward the door.

"Sunny, last question. What was the boy's father's name?"

"Jimmy Richards. His son's name was Allen. Mr. Richards owns a small hardware store near that new development just south of Cedar Bay. I don't know his wife's name. Now, I really do need to go, but if you think of anything else you'd like to ask me, just call the school. Thanks again, and I need a bill for lunch."

"No charge, Sunny. This one's on me. That's the least I can do for monopolizing your lunch hour. Hope to see you soon."

"You know you will. For some reason, those salads of Charlie's always have my name on them."

"I'll let him know, and I'm sure it will make his day. Again, thanks."

CHAPTER THIRTEEN

Kelly locked up the coffee shop at two that afternoon and went home to pick up Rebel before she headed out to the nursing home. When Kelly had been given Skyy, she and Mike discussed what would happen if the county health inspector ever came to Kelly's Koffee Shop and found two or three dogs on the premises. Occasionally Mike took one of the older dogs to work with him, but they decided they had to come up with a better plan. Given the fact that Mike was the county sheriff, it wouldn't look good for him to have a wife who was stretching the law by having dogs in a public place where food was served, even if it was the storeroom.

The solution came in the form of a doggie door they had built into the garage door that led to the fenced back yard, so the dogs could freely go in and out. Their dog beds were in the garage, and since Mike left the house later than Kelly and she returned earlier than him, the dogs were only on their own for five or six hours.

When Kelly got home from work she greeted the dogs, let them outside, and then put Lady and Skyy in the garage, motioning for Rebel to follow her. Although he was perfectly trained she decided to take a leash since having him in a nursing home was a new experience for both of them.

She drove the short distance to the nursing home and parked in the visitor's lot, snapping the leash on Rebel's collar when they got out of her minivan. They walked through the door and over to the reception desk.

"Hi, my name's Kelly Reynolds, and this is Rebel. We're here to see the director, Janet Bryce."

"Welcome. Mrs. Bryce told me she was expecting you. I'll call her and let her know you're here."

A few moments later the door to the office behind the reception desk opened, and a smiling grey-haired grandmotherly looking woman walked towards Kelly and Rebel. "Hi, I'm Janet Bryce. Please call me Janet." She reached down with her hand and patted Rebel on the head.

"Thank you so much for coming. As I told Roxie, this is a new experience for us, but according to the article I read in the journal, dogs often have a calming effect on patients, and with what some of the people here are going through, I thought it was worth a try. Follow me, and I'll take you to Nancy Wilson's room." She led them down a hall and stopped outside a door with the name "Nancy Wilson" taped on it.

"Janet, what do you want Rebel to do?" Kelly asked.

"I really don't have anything planned. Maybe we could talk to Nancy, and Rebel could sit next to her. I'll assure her that he's friendly, and let's see how she responds."

Janet knocked on the door and when a voice said, "Please come in," the three of them entered a room filled with late afternoon sunlight.

"Nancy, I mentioned to you this morning that Mrs. Reynolds was going to bring her dog in to see you today. Your friend Roxie works for her, and she's the one who suggested it. Is it all right with you if he sits down next to your chair?"

"Yes, I'd like that. When I was growing up we always had dogs, but my husband was allergic to them and after he died, I just never got around to getting another one. What's his name?"

"It's Rebel, Mrs. Wilson. Rebel, come," Kelly said walking over to where Mrs. Wilson was sitting in a chair. "Sit, Rebel."

Rebel sat next to the chair, and Mrs. Wilson reached her hand out and patted his head. Rebel put a paw on her lap and looked up at her as if to say, "Don't stop petting me."

"Janet, I wish you'd read that article a couple of weeks ago. I'd forgotten how good it feels to have a friend that doesn't require anything more from you than a pat on the head. I'm sorry I don't have any treats to give him." She looked down and said, "What a good boy, you are, Rebel."

Kelly reached into her purse, took out a small plastic bag, and handed it to Nancy. "I have three dogs, so I always carry a few treats in my purse. He has a very gentle mouth, so don't worry about him suddenly grabbing one of the treats away from you."

Nancy handed Rebel the treats and Janet smiled. The three of them talked for several minutes, and then Janet looked at her watch. "Nancy, I'm afraid we have to leave. I cleared having Rebel spend some time with you, but your doctor said the one thing we weren't to do was tire you out."

"I'm not the least bit tired. If anything, I feel the best I've felt since I came here." She turned to Kelly and said, "Please bring him again. He makes me happy."

"With all the treats you just gave Rebel, I don't think you'll have to ask him twice. If it's all right with you, Janet, we can come back next week."

"It's fine with me. I'm wondering if I should ask a few of the other patients if they'd enjoy being around a dog, say maybe five or so."

"Since I'm the test case here, I think I should be allowed to have him all to myself for a few minutes before I share him with any of the others. After all it was my friend who set this up," Nancy said, laughing

"We'll be here next week, and we'll be happy to see some of the other patients, won't we, Rebel?" Kelly asked.

The big dog licked Nancy's hand, and Kelly could swear she saw a tear in the corner of her eye. "Rebel, come. Say goodbye to Mrs. Wilson." Rebel licked her hand again and walked to the door with Kelly and Janet. "See you next week," Kelly said to Nancy.

CHAPTER FOURTEEN

Janet shut the door to Nancy Wilson's room, and they started walking down the hall to the entrance. "Kelly, Rebel, thank you so much. That was definitely a success. It's so generous of both of you to share your time with us. If there's anything I can do for you, please let me know."

"Actually, Janet, there is. I believe you have a woman convalescing here by the name of Linda Devine. I wonder if it would be possible for me to talk to her for a few minutes. If you'd prefer, I can put Rebel in my minivan."

"Absolutely not. I'm sure Linda would enjoy him as much as Nancy did. She's down this hall. Let me go in first. Is there something I should tell her?"

"You can tell her I'm a friend of the woman who was her principal when she was teaching, Sunny Jacobs."

A few minutes later Janet opened the door to the room and motioned Kelly and Rebel in. "Linda, I'd like you to meet Kelly Reynolds and her dog, Rebel."

Kelly walked over to the woman and shook her hand while Rebel sat next to her, looking up at her. "Please have a seat in that chair. Rebel, you can stay next to me," she said as she reached down and patted his head. "How is Sunny doing? I haven't seen her for a while."

"She's fine. I had lunch with her today. Actually, I own Kelly's Koffee Shop, and she's a pretty regular customer of ours."

"Yes, I remember her talking about it one time. How can I help you?" she asked, continuing to pet Rebel who had put a paw on her lap.

"I assume you know Maggie Ryan was murdered the day before yesterday," Kelly said. Linda nodded with a sad look on her face. "My husband is Mike Reynolds, the sheriff of Beaver County. He's investigating her murder, and I understand she was a friend of yours. I'd appreciate anything you could tell me about her. Mike isn't having much luck finding motives or suspects. Since you were her friend, I thought I'd see if you could help."

Linda was quiet for several moments. "I've been afraid for months something like this would happen," she said looking out the window while she folded and refolded her hands.

"Why do you say that?" Kelly asked.

"Kelly, Linda, I have a few things I need to do. I'm going to have to excuse myself, if you don't mind. I'll be in my office," Janet said as she walked out the door.

Linda turned to Kelly and said, "I used to visit Maggie weekly. Actually, I was the one who took most of her groceries to her. She also had several deliveries a week from Meals on Wheels. Over the last few years, she changed. She told me two years ago that she'd started getting a lot of telephone calls, but when she answered the phone no one was there. I could tell it was concerning her. About that time, she started to adopt dogs from different dog adoption agencies, some as far away as Portland. She told them she would pay for their time and gas if they would deliver the dogs to her along with a large bag of dog food."

"I wondered how she could get that many dogs, and no one in Cedar Bay seemed to know about it," Kelly said. "That explains it."

"She never told me outright, but I think she became spooked by the telephone calls and got the dogs as protection. I really don't know what else it could have been. When she was teaching, she used to have a weekly share-a- pet day where the children brought in pictures of their pet to pin on the classroom bulletin board. She once told me she could never understand how some families could have more than one pet, but it seemed like every time I went to her home, she'd gotten another dog. I know she hired someone from one of the adoption agencies to come out to her home and clean up her yard twice a week. She told me she paid them well."

"Given what I've been told about her health, I wondered how she cared for them," Kelly said. "That explains that part, and it would make sense if she was frightened for her personal safety to protect herself with lots of dogs."

"Yes," Linda said, "but obviously, it didn't work. What I don't understand is how anyone got in her house and murdered her. I would have thought the dogs would scare away whoever it was. I saw on the television news that the dogs were taken to the Cedar Bay Animal Shelter."

"Yes, I helped the director take the dogs over there. She's trying to get people to adopt them or at least foster them, because this is a big drain on the shelter's finances."

"I wonder if she knows that Maggie left her estate to them."

"How did you know that, Linda? I don't think her will has been filed for probate yet."

"Maggie told me several months ago she'd changed her will and left everything to them, because she knew when something happened to her that the dogs would probably be taken there, and she felt she needed to do something to help them."

"She certainly was thinking ahead, and that was a very generous thing for her to do."

"I agree. She told me she'd made a prior will and left everything to Reverend Barnes. Evidently he'd asked her to leave it to him, so he could make the decisions about where it would best be spent at the church. She said he didn't want to be bogged down by any of the church committees haggling over how the money should be used. She also mentioned he had kind of strong-armed her to do that."

"In what fashion? That hardly sounds like something the minister of a church would do."

"I agree, and I asked her the same question. She told me that while she'd always been religious, as she'd gotten older she'd become more concerned about whether or not she'd go to heaven. He told her the only way someone could be certain they'd go to heaven was if they left their estate to a church. He even told her if she did that, he'd come to her house twice a week and they would pray for her to go to heaven when she died. Reverend Barnes gave her the names of quite a few famous people who had done just that, left their estate to the minister of their church. That's when she made her will out and named him as her beneficiary."

"Linda, I can't thank you enough for telling all of this to me. I know we're wearing out our welcome here, but I do have one other question I'd like to ask you."

"Certainly, and you've brought so much joy to my day by bringing Rebel with you. Will he be coming back?"

"Yes, we'll be here next week. What can you tell me about a student of Maggie's named Allen Richards and his father?"

Linda was quiet for several moments and then told her essentially what Sunny had said earlier that day. "I think in her heart of hearts, Maggie lived in fear that he somehow blamed her for Allen making a mess of his life, although that was ridiculous. Maggie was a wonderful teacher, and her students' best interests were always at the forefront of whatever she did. She honestly felt it was in Allen's best interest to be held back a year. She told me once she was just sorry that his kindergarten or first grade teacher hadn't held him back. It would have made the following years for him much easier."

"When I heard about the incident, I wondered the same thing. Why do you think he wasn't held back earlier?"

"Teachers are under a lot of pressure to have their students matriculate to the next grade, both by the school system and the parents. Teachers are made to feel like failures if children are held back, like they didn't do their job properly. Even though it would be far better in many cases, it's rarely done. In this case, I think the child was just a bad apple to start with.

"I know Maggie always felt a sense of failure over the way Allen ended up, but I think the fact he went on to a different school system and the next grade and still had so many problems illustrated clearly that what she had tried to do for him was the right thing. Unfortunately, his father refused to accept that there might be something wrong with his son. He chose to believe it was just Maggie wanting to hold him back. I understand that after all these years, he still resents it."

"Even though Maggie Ryan was my teacher and my children's teacher, I hadn't seen her for years, but it sounds like her later years were not particularly happy ones," Kelly said.

"I'd have to agree with you. I don't know if any of this will help your husband solve the case, but I certainly hope so. She may have been a bit odd in her later years, but no one deserves to die like she did. I don't think that woman had a cruel or mean bone in her body."

"Thank you so much. Rebel, come. Linda, we'll see you next week and hopefully, Mike will have found her murderer by then. Again, thanks for your help."

CHAPTER FIFTEEN

Kelly left the nursing home with her mind buzzing. Rebel had definitely been a hit, but she never doubted that he wouldn't be. She was anxious to tell Mike what she'd found out about the reverend and also about Jimmy Richards. Nancy Wilson's account of the Richards incident several years ago certainly dovetailed with what Sunny had told her earlier in the day.

On her way home, she remembered she needed to buy some coffee and fresh fruit at the market. Mike had read that granola with fruit was a very healthy way to start the day, so he'd started making his own granola mixing together rolled oats, crushed cashews, raisins, and an organic granola he'd purchased online. To that he added yogurt and fresh fruit. He'd told Kelly on numerous occasions that he had far more energy and felt much better since he'd started beginning his days with it.

After she'd parked her minivan in the parking lot of the market she turned in her seat and said, "Rebel, stay. I'll be back in a few minutes." She partly rolled down the windows, and as soon as she'd closed her door, Rebel got in the passenger seat, letting everyone who passed by the minivan know that it was well guarded.

When Kelly was checking her cart to make sure she'd gotten all the fruits Mike wanted, she heard someone say, "Kelly, it's good to see you. Actually, I was going to give you a call. Do you have a few minutes to talk?"

Kelly looked up and said, "Hi, Mary. Of course I have time for you. Let's get a cup of coffee and sit down. I'll meet you at the coffee shop in the rear of the store."

Mary was the secretary at the Church of Loving Grace, the Reverend Barnes' church, and they'd become friends over the years. Mary was a frequent lunchtime customer at the coffee shop.

A few minutes later they sat down with a hot cup of coffee. When Kelly looked closely at Mary, she noticed the deep worry lines etched on her face, and said, "What's wrong, Mary?"

Mary was quiet for several moments as she looked down at her coffee and then she said, "Kelly, I don't know where to begin, but I have a very bad feeling about something, and I just can't keep it to myself any longer."

"I have a big ear, so why don't you start at the beginning?"

"All right," Mary said. She took a sip of her coffee and began to speak. "Kelly, you know I'm the secretary at the Church of Loving Grace. I've been there for almost ten years, and I not only like the interaction with the parishioners, I really like Reverend Barnes."

"I don't see any problem there," Kelly said. "From the way you're blushing, I'm wondering if perhaps you have some romantic feelings towards him."

Mary was quiet for several moments. "Let's just say we've spent a lot of time together, particularly recently. He likes my cooking, and he's indicated maybe it's time he found a wife. You know my husband died at a pretty young age, and I'm tired of being a widow. I definitely have developed feelings for him, but I'm concerned about a few things."

"Like what?" Kelly asked.

"Well, even before we became, how should I say this, better friends, he and I had always gotten along very well. We've never kept secrets from one another. By that I mean he was always free to help himself to the candy I keep in my desk drawer or look at my computer to see what I was working on, and I pretty much did the same. When he went to lunch, I'd critique the sermons he composed on his computer, you know, that type of openness."

"From what you're saying, I'm gathering that's changed."

"Yes," Mary said. "Several months ago Reverend Barnes started locking his office when he left for lunch and instead of me looking at his sermons during the lunch hour, he'd call me in specifically and have me look at them. It was as if he no longer trusted me. One time I asked him why he'd started locking his door, and he said he'd been told it wasn't a good idea for the church leader to leave his office unlocked because often there were confidential things about parishioners in it, and someone might use that information inappropriately. I thought it was a little strange, but there was some validity to what he said. He assured me he trusted me."

"I can see the logic there. It's kind of a stretch to think something like that could happen in our sleepy little town, but I suppose erring on the side of caution is not a bad thing for the leader of the church to do," Kelly said.

"When I started thinking about it, I realized that something else had happened several months prior to his locking the door. There was a woman who used to attend church regularly, Maggie Ryan, but she became unable to attend when her osteoporosis got really bad. She couldn't drive any longer. There were a couple of years she didn't attend church at all, although she would call Reverend Barnes from time to time to talk to him. About six months ago he started going to her house twice a week to pray with her."

"Did he usually go to the homes of parishioners to pray with them?" Kelly asked.

"Not to my knowledge. Sure, there were times when someone

died or a crisis happened, and he'd go to the family home to console them or pray with them, but never on a regular basis. This became something he did twice every week, no matter what. He told me Maggie was a very religious woman, and it was the least he could do for her."

"Mary, nothing you've told me so far indicates a red flag. While those two things may not be the norm for a church leader, they don't seem to indicate a real problem."

"No, but let me finish. After a couple of months of going to Maggie's home Reverend Barnes told me she was so grateful for what he was doing for her, she'd decided to leave her estate to him."

"Again, I wouldn't say that was unusual," Kelly said realizing that Mary was unaware that Maggie Ryan had recently changed her will.

"No, it's not, but here's where it gets unusual. One day two months ago Reverend Barnes had to leave his office unexpectedly when a parishioner had been in a bad accident. The man's wife had called and asked the reverend to meet them at the hospital. When I walked down the hall to the restroom I walked by his office, and even though his computer faced away from the doorway leading to his office, I saw a glowing light that indicated he'd forgotten to turn off his computer. Our church doesn't have a lot of extra money, so we're all very careful to never waste electricity. I went into his office to turn his computer off, and I couldn't believe what was displayed on his computer." She put her head in her hands and began to quietly cry.

"Mary, what was on his computer that was so awful?" Kelly asked even though she was pretty sure what the answer was going to be.

"It was a gambling site, which by itself wouldn't have been so bad. What was bad was it had the amount of money Reverend Barnes owed to them. He owed $37,500." She sat back and looked at Kelly.

"There's more, isn't there?" Kelly said.

"Yes, even now I can't believe I did what I did." She put her head in her hands again.

"Mary, I'm sure whatever you did you felt you had to do at the time. What was it?"

"I searched his desk drawers, and I found a piece of paper with several websites written on it. I pulled all of them up on the computer. I found out that Reverend Barnes owed different internet gambling sites over $200,000." She took a sip of her coffee. "I never told him what I'd found. I didn't even turn off the computer, because I didn't want him to know I'd been in his office. Later, when we were together, I just pretended nothing had happened, but I've really been torn up about it."

"I'm sure you know that Maggie Ryan was recently murdered," Kelly said.

"Yes. What I've told you so far is bad enough, but here's the worst part. Reverend Barnes had an appointment early this afternoon with Lem Bates, the attorney, regarding Maggie Ryan's will. I usually don't work on Wednesday afternoons, but one of the parishioners had given me a recipe for a stew she'd made at the last church social, and I'd left it in my office. I thought I'd make it for dinner tonight, since he was planning on coming over.

"Sorry, Kelly, I know I'm rambling. Anyway, I went back to the church and walked down the hall to my office. It was three this afternoon. Reverend Barnes' door was closed, but I could hear his voice. I put my ear next to the door and heard him crying and apparently muttering to himself."

"Could you make out what he was saying?" Kelly asked.

"It was indistinct, but I think I heard him say the words 'It was all for nothing. I did it for nothing. She left everything to the animal shelter. I don't believe it.' Like I said, it was hard for me to understand what he was saying, but I think that was it."

"Mary, why did you want to tell me all of this?"

"The reverend told me your husband was in charge of Maggie's murder investigation, and I thought he should know about this. I feel like I'm being completely disloyal to Reverend Barnes, but Kelly, I'm so scared. What if he was the one who murdered Maggie? What if I'm in love with a murderer? I can't believe it, but it all makes sense now. He needed the money, and she'd willed everything to him. When I heard him talking to himself it all seemed to fit. I was going to call you. It's just a coincidence I saw you in here today."

Kelly reached over and patted Mary's hand. "Mary, there's nothing I can say that's going to make you feel any better about this situation, but I will tell Mike everything you've told me. Maybe there's a simple explanation, although I don't think there's any denying that Reverend Barnes would have to be considered a suspect. Believe me, if Mike talks to him, and he probably will have to, your name will never be mentioned.

"Go on home and act as if nothing ever happened. If he's not the murderer, he's going to need you to help him get through this gambling addiction and the debt. If he is the murderer, you'll have to make a decision regarding what your relationship will be with him in the future. That's a decision only you can make. It's out of your hands now, and you absolutely did the right thing by telling me."

Kelly looked at her watch. "I need to leave now. It's much later than I thought and probably too late for you to start a stew. I'll let you know what happens."

"Do you think I should have him over tonight for dinner? I don't really know what to do now."

"Like I said, it's out of your hands. Have him over for dinner, go into work tomorrow, and do what you usually do. Really, there's nothing you can do for now. You certainly don't want to falsely accuse him. Thanks for having the courage to tell me all of this. I'll be talking to you."

As Kelly walked out to her minivan, her mind was a jumble of thoughts, and she knew she needed to share them with Mike. She'd just secured her seatbelt when her phone rang. The screen showed Roxie's name.

"Hi, Roxie. Hope you're not calling me to tell me you can't come to work tomorrow. I'll understand if you can't, but as busy as we've been, you'd really be missed." She heard crying and said, "Roxie, what's wrong? What's happened?"

"It's Betsy, Kelly, that German shepherd dog we were going to adopt. I told you Dr. Simpson said he was going to take some more X-rays today, and they showed that she has a large tumor."

"Take a deep breath, Roxie. Lots of dogs have tumors that can be successfully removed. What did he say?"

Roxie was crying softly, and it took her a few moments to speak. "He took a sample of the tumor, and it's malignant. He said sometimes tumors such as the one she has can be removed. He's going to operate early tomorrow morning. I was thinking of going to his clinic while he operated on her, but in reality, that's probably stupid. I couldn't do anything anyway, and I've only been around her once."

"I agree. Since it's after hours, I imagine no one is answering the clinic's phone, but I know they have an answering machine. Why don't you leave a message that you'd like to come tomorrow when she gets out of surgery? I think it would do you more good than her for you to see Betsy. Who knows? She might recognize you, and it might make her recovery a little easier. We'll do without you at the coffee shop for however long it takes. I think that would work."

"Thanks, Kelly. I knew you'd understand and that would probably be much better than sitting in his waiting room, when I don't really have a relationship with the dog. See you in the morning."

Kelly ended the call and thought, not for the first time, how easy it is for a dog to wend its way into someone's heart in a matter of seconds. Barring any problems, she knew Roxie's family would be providing a very good home for Betsy. She crossed her fingers for luck, an old childhood habit, and hoped she was right.

CHAPTER SIXTEEN

Mike knocked on the door of the Shannon and Ralph Lewis household, hoping they'd remembered something about Maggie Ryan since he'd talked to them yesterday.

The door was cautiously opened and Mike saw a woman peering through the narrow opening. "Yeah, Sheriff, what can I do for ya'? Don't know nothin' since we talked yesterday, but thanks fer comin'. If Ralphie or me remembers something, we'll call you, like we said we would yesterday."

"Mrs. Lewis, may I come in for a moment? I need to ask you some questions. I'd prefer to do it this way, rather than have one of my deputies bring you in for questioning. It won't take long, I promise."

"Yer' the one holdin' all the cards, Sheriff. Come on in." She opened the door for him, turned around, and yelled, "Ralphie, got us some company. That sheriff from yesterday has come back. He wants to talk to us." She turned back to Mike and said, "Ralphie'll be here in a minute. He's just finishin' up his lunch. You can have a seat over there." She pointed to a chair that was upholstered in shades of brown, but it was hard to tell what the original color had been from all of the spots and stains.

The television blared the latest stock market numbers as Shannon stared at it. "Sorry, Sheriff, be with ya' in a minute, but need to see what my stocks are doin'. We got purty much everything we own, other than this house, invested in the market, and it ain't lookin' real good today."

A few moments later an elderly man shuffled into the room wearing a good part of the contents of his lunch on the front of his denim shirt which was badly in need of a visit to the washing machine. He walked over to Mike and put his hand out. "Afternoon, Sheriff. Caught the guy who did it to Miss Ryan yet?"

"Unfortunately, no. That's why I'm here. I'm hoping that one of you has thought of something that might shed some light on this case. Anything you can remember that might seem unusual could help me."

"What did ya' say, Sheriff? Couldn't here ya'," Shannon said.

"It might help if you put the television on mute. It's probably hard to hear me over it. I asked if you'd thought of anything since I was here yesterday."

"Can't say that I have, Sheriff," she said after she'd turned the television to mute. "Can't think of anything different or somethin' we would have noticed. What's gonna happen to all them dogs she had?"

"They've been taken to the Cedar Bay Animal Shelter. Several of them have been adopted, and some others have been placed with foster families until there's a little more space at the shelter," Mike answered and then he said, "Mrs. Lewis, you mentioned you watch the stock market on TV, right?"

"Yeah, it's kind of my hobby. Like to see how my money's doin,' ya' know?"

"I've never gotten involved in the market, but it occurs to me if you spend a lot of time in this room watching the stock market, you'd probably be aware if something strange was going on over at Miss Ryan's home. I noticed you have a clear vision of her house from the front window here in your living room. I'd like you to think back to the last week or so and tell me what you noticed going on over there."

"Shannon'd know better than anyone. Spends half her time lookin' out the front window at the Ryan home, don't ya' Shannon?" Ralph said.

"I do not," she said bristling. "Jes' sometimes I'd see vans pullin' up to the gate, and I knew that infernal barkin' was gonna get worse, and darned if every time it didn't."

"So, you saw some dogs being delivered, is that right?" Mike asked.

"Nah, can't say I saw the actual dogs. What I saw was the vans that brought them in, leastways I think that's what happened. They always drove behind the house, and I couldn't see what was actually in the vans, but since the barkin' jes' kept gettin' worse and worse, thinkin' that's what happened."

"How long have you lived here?" Mike asked them.

"Goin' on twelve years. I remember because we moved in here jes' after I retired from the factory down in Coos Bay. Always kinda liked Cedar Bay, and we decided to move here. Got us a good deal on the house cuz the previous owner died here and his kids didn't want nothin' to do with it other than to get their hands on the money from sellin' it," Ralph said.

"In the twelve years you've lived here, did either one of you ever meet Maggie Ryan?"

"Nah. We used to see her go to work when we first moved here. Heard she was a teacher, but then I guess she retired, and the only time we'd see her was when she went to the mailbox out by the gate once in a while," Ralph said.

"Did she have many visitors?" Mike asked.

"Shannon can probably answer that cuz she's the one whose always lookin' out the window."

She gave Ralph a dirty look and said, "Once in awhile when I'd hear somethin' unusual, I'd look out the window to see what it was. A woman usually visited her about once a week and a man, I think he might be a preacher, came twice a week. A coupla times I seen one of them 'Meals on Wheels' trucks, so I figger she was havin' some food delivered. That's about it."

"You mentioned the dogs barking a lot. Did they bark at specific times?" Mike asked.

"Like clockwork in the mornin' and evenin' even though she kept them in the house most of the time. Always figgered they was hungry for breakfast and dinner. There was also some guy that would come twice a week and stay for about half an hour or so. I'd see him walkin' around the yard with a bag. Maybe he was pickin' up dog stuff. Many dogs as that ol' lady had, must have been a real mess."

"Did either one of you hear the dogs bark at strange times, like in the middle of the night?"

"Yeah, Shannon, remember? Couple of times lately we was waked up by them dogs."

"How could I forget it? Don't know how many times that old lady's dogs woke me up. Can't even count the number of times I'd wake up in the mornin' so tired I could barely keep my eyes open to watch the stock market. Usually took me a little nap when the market closed on the days when that happened. Don't wish a bad death on anyone, but in her case, with all the dogs she had yappin' and barkin' all the time, might be some kind of cosmic justice. Jes' sayin'."

"The night before last, the night she was murdered, did you hear anything suspicious? Were the dogs barking at an unusual time?"

"Nah, but now that I think 'bout it, I was lookin' out the window wondering when they were gonna stop, when I seen a man dressed in black kinda hurryin' along the street. Ya' know, this neighborhood's too old fer street lights and sidewalks, but I do 'member thinkin' it was odd that someone would be out walkin' in the street when it was dark outside."

"Mrs. Lewis, can you tell me anything else? Are you sure it was a man? How tall do you think he was? Could you see his face? Was he fat or thin? Anything you could tell me might help."

She was quiet for a few long moments and then she said, "I'm not much good with stuff like that, but he was a little taller than you. He wasn't fat and he wasn't thin, kinda normal, ya' know? It definitely was a man. He didn't have no hat on, and I could kinda make out his face. That's why I said it was a man."

"Could you identify him if you ever saw him again?" Mike asked.

"Nah, it was too dark. Jes' purty sure it was a man, but other than that, can't tell ya' nothin'."

"Well, Sheriff, maybe Shannon lookin' out at the street at the old lady's house all the time'll help ya'."

"Thanks for taking the time to talk to me. If you think of anything else, please call me. I think I gave you my card with my number on it the night of the murder, but here's another one for you. I'll let you get back to the stock market."

"It's okay, Sheriff. Been watchin' with one eye, and it looks like it's a little bit up now. Think we made a little money today." She looked at the clock on the wall and said, "Ralphie, mailman'll be here in a minute. You know how prompt he is. Comes at 3:30 every day. You can set your clock on it. I'm going out to the mailbox. I'm expectin' some information on a stock I'm thinkin' of buyin' fer us," she said, following Mike out as he opened the door.

Wonder if she really saw anyone. Sounds like she really hated those dogs. Wonder if she hated them enough to murder Maggie Ryan.

CHAPTER SEVENTEEN

Mike had turned off his phone while he'd been at the Lewis home. He checked his messages once he was in his car ready to go back to the station. There were two. One was from the Fire Chief, Wayne Rogers, and the other one was from the attorney, Lem Bates. He pulled away from the curb and called Chief Rogers on his Bluetooth.

"Chief Rogers here," the voice on the other end of the call said.

"Hi, Wayne, it's Mike Reynolds. Sorry I missed your call, but I was talking to some people who I sense are a little skittish of law enforcement personnel, and I didn't want any distractions. Do you have something for me?"

"Given the number of dogs in the Ryan household, I'm not sure this is relevant, but my department did some more testing today on what we found in the house, and there was an unusually large amount of meat byproducts."

"Chief, what do you mean by that? You lost me."

"We're pretty sure the byproducts came from dog treats, and Mike, there was a lot of meat byproduct material in the bags of possible DNA material we took from the house. As a matter of fact, I had two of my men go back out there today and vacuum the kitchen, the living room, as well as the bedroom where we found the decedent's body. They filled several bags with dog hair and more meat byproducts."

"All right, what do you think that means? Does it have anything to do with the fire or the murder?" Mike asked.

"Not precisely. Here's my thinking on it. We know Maggie Ryan had over thirty dogs in the house. I find it hard to believe a couple of them, maybe a lot more than that, would allow a stranger to come in the house and murder the person who fed them. That part has bothered me from when we first found the body. I think whoever did it enticed the dogs with dog treats, and that's where all the byproducts we found came from. If my thinking is correct, it means a couple of things. Are you with me?" the chief asked.

"I am, but I've never heard of anything like this."

"We know the dogs were in the house when the murder was committed because your deputy, Brandon Wynn, let them out when he got there. My thinking is what better way to get in a house than giving the dogs huge amounts of treats. Amounts large enough that the dogs would be distracted and not notice someone going in the bedroom and murdering their master."

"That's a plausible theory. What's the second thing?" Mike asked.

"If someone brought that amount of dog treats into a house, he or she had to know there were a lot of dogs in the house. To me, that means that the person was known to the decedent or had been there before. Think about it Mike. No one would randomly go into a house that had that number of dogs in it unless they had a plan."

"And you're saying the plan was to distract the dogs with the dog treats, so he or she could murder their owner. You're also saying there was nothing random about the murder or the fire."

"Yes. I don't think we can come up with the brand of dog treats, because the byproducts were pretty generic, so although I certainly am not telling you how to do your job, but if it was me, I'd start looking at who would know how many dogs she had, in other words, someone known to her."

"Since we didn't find any signs of forcible entry, I'd have to agree with you."

"Wish I could tell you our tests came up with the name of the murderer, but that didn't happen. Good luck on this one, Mike. It's really bizarre."

"My sentiments exactly, Chief. Thanks for the input."

"No problem. Keep me in the loop," he said before ending the call.

As in all cases, one thing led to another, and in this case, it looked like a dog treat was the reason the murder was allowed to take place. While he was mulling it over, Mike remembered Lem had called. He called him and a moment later heard his secretary say, "Lem Bates' office. May I help you?"

"This is Sheriff Reynolds. I'm returning Lem's call."

"Good to hear from you, Sheriff. I'll tell Lem you're on the line."

"Mike, thanks for getting back to me so quickly," Lem said when he got on the line.

"Not a problem, Lem. I'm assuming this has something to do with your meeting with Reverend Barnes. Would I be right?"

"That you would be. It was interesting and went pretty much like I thought it would go. After the niceties were over, he told me he was there to begin the probate proceedings for Maggie Ryan's will. He took the will he had from his briefcase and handed it to me. It was the old will which named him as the beneficiary."

"What did you do then?"

"After I made a point of studying it I told him, that yes, at one time that had been Maggie's will, but she had executed a newer one, and the will he had was voided by the subsequent will. I had the newer will on my desk and showed it to him and pointed out the date Maggie Ryan had executed it and told him that my secretary and I had acted as witnesses."

"How did he take it?" Mike asked.

"He was shocked. He couldn't believe she'd drawn up a new will and never told him about it. He kept saying, 'But I went over there twice a week. How could she do this to me?' It was as if he felt he had a right to her estate, and that he had been counting on it. And Mike, the thing that's been bothering me ever since this came up is that in the first will Maggie Ryan named him, not the Church of Loving Grace, as the beneficiary of her will. I asked him about that."

Mike interrupted Lem, "How did he answer?"

"He said he'd told Maggie it was better for him to do it that way, so he could give her money to church projects without having to go through various church committees to get approval."

"Lem, you're the lawyer, not me. Have you ever drawn up a will, before or since, that named an individual person as a beneficiary with the intent being that the beneficiary would give it to a charitable organization such as a church?"

"Never, and here's the interesting thing. I didn't draw up the first will. I was on vacation when it was drawn up by an attorney over in Jackson who was filling in for me while my wife and I were away. I looked at the work he'd done when I got back, but there was so much for me to absorb I didn't think much about it. I filed it and when I drew up her new will, I thought it was rather strange, but I decided she'd told the lawyer filling in for me that's what she wanted to do. If I'd drawn it up, I would have questioned it. Mike, I'm not particularly suspicious by nature..."

"Lem, as I said earlier, you're a lawyer. Of course you're

TROUBLE AT THE ANIMAL SHELTER

suspicious, but go ahead."

"Thanks, Mike, I'll make sure I remember the next law enforcement joke I'm told, so I can tell it to you. Anyway, I was left with the impression that he was panicked. I don't know what his situation is, but I got the feeling he was devastated by the news, far more than the situation warranted. Sure, it meant that his church might not be able to do some projects he felt were important, but it seemed to be more personal than that. I don't like to think of a man of the cloth having ulterior motives in a situation like this, but I have to tell you that's what I'm thinking."

"I appreciate your telling me this, and like you, I have no idea what his situation is, but I think I better find out. I'll let you know if I find out anything. One more thing, Lem. Is it okay with you if I tell the people out at the animal shelter about Maggie Ryan's will?"

"Yes, actually that will save me a trip. I started the probate proceedings this afternoon by filing her will with the court, so it's public knowledge now."

Mike had one more stop to make before he went home. He needed to tell the Cedar Bay Animal Shelter that it is going to be the recipient of Maggie Ryan's estate.

CHAPTER EIGHTEEN

Mike parked his car in the visitor's parking lot at the animal shelter and was glad to see the lot was almost full. He was hopeful it meant a lot of people were adopting or fostering the dogs that had been brought over from Maggie Ryan's home.

He knocked on the door that had the word "Office" stenciled on it and heard a female voice say, "Come in." He walked into the small office and saw Jenna Lee sitting at her desk. They'd met from time to time over the years and had waved to each other at the Ryan home when Kelly had been helping Jenna transport the dogs to the shelter.

"Sheriff, it's good to see you. At least I prefer seeing you here rather than the way we met the other night. Please, have a seat," she said gesturing to the chair across from her desk.

"Jenna, I'm hoping from how crowded the parking lot is that you're getting a lot of people to come in and look at the new rescues."

"We've been lucky. Kelly announced it at the coffee shop yesterday, and the newspaper and our local radio station have really been great about helping us get the word out. The good news is that almost half the dogs we brought in from the Ryan home have been fostered or adopted. Now if we can just make it through the next few days. I'm playing a game of Russian roulette with our finances here.

82

We're always hard up for money. In fact, I'm the only paid employee, and if my husband didn't support us, I couldn't afford to work here. To say I'm paid a small salary would be an overstatement."

She ran her hand through her thick dark hair and said, "Fortunately I love dogs. Always have and always will. I'm just a sucker for them. There's something about helping a living thing who only wants affection from you that keeps me going. These animals don't have voices, so I've pretty much become their spokesman, or spokeswoman, if that's the more politically correct thing to say. I simply can't understand how anyone could abandon their pet. I know some animals get lost or escape through an open gate, but I think they're in the minority, and those are usually the ones whose owners find them within a day. I'm scared to death we're going to have to close this shelter because of the influx of all these dogs."

She paused and then continued, "It's not just the number of dogs that we have and how much money it costs to feed them. I found out last week that our water pipes are leaking. The plumber I called to look at them said they need to be replaced as soon as possible, or they'd burst. He gave me a quote of $10,000. There is no way I can afford to have them repaired. We simply don't have the money."

"I'm glad you're sitting down, Jenna, because I think what I'm going to tell you is going to make your life a lot easier, and certainly make the lives of the dogs you care for a lot easier."

She looked at him, obviously confused by what he was saying. "Mike, I don't have any idea what you're talking about."

"I'm not surprised. I just talked to Lem Bates, and he said I could tell you that Maggie Ryan left her entire estate to the Cedar Bay Animal Shelter, and so saying, I rather imagine I just made your day."

She looked at him in shock for several moments and then began to cry. "I've been praying for a miracle, and this is it. I can't believe it," she said as tears ran down her cheeks. She reached into her desk drawer and pulled out a box of Kleenex.

Mike gave her some time to digest what he'd just told her and then said, "Jenna, it gets better. Maggie lived in the old farmhouse that had been in her family ever since they'd come to Cedar Bay. She has no relatives, and since she never had to buy furniture or pay for the house, she invested her money, and from what Lem told me, quiet wisely. Evidently the only thing she spent money on was her dogs. He told me with the sale of the house, and as you saw, there was some damage to it from the fire, but not much, it seems the estate will be just a little under a million dollars."

He watched as her jaw dropped in amazement. Tears continued to run down her cheeks and soon they turned dark from being mixed with the mascara she wore. She made no attempt to brush them away. It was as if she was incapable of doing anything but continuing to look at Mike with a shocked expression on her face.

"Sheriff, I'm sorry, but I never expected anything like this. It's the most wonderful thing that's ever happened. I guess she really liked dogs, and that's why she left it to us. Do you know anything more?"

"No, Lem and I think she knew if anything happened to her, the dogs would be brought here. And I'd also bet she knew that you didn't have the funds to care for thirty additional dogs. Did she ever adopt a dog from here?"

"No, the first I knew about her dogs was when I got the call from your deputy."

"Well, that doesn't surprise me. She probably felt this shelter was too close to home and worried that someone might discover she was way over the three dog limit and would report her to the county authorities."

"Mike, do you have any idea when we might get the money from the estate?"

"None. Why don't you call Lem Bates? He can give you the details and Jenna, I'm really happy the shelter is going to get the money. You do a wonderful job here on a shoestring, and now you'll have a chance to do some things you've probably wanted to do for a long time."

"My head is spinning," she said and then laughed. "Do you have any idea how happy this is going to make my husband? I know he was worried I was going to take the money for the water pipes here at the shelter out of our personal savings account. Not only did you make my day, or rather my year, you made my husband's as well. Thank you so much."

"Thank Maggie Ryan. She's the one who did it. Kind of sad she'll never get to see the result of naming the shelter as the sole beneficiary of her will, but I guess none of us ever gets to see what happens when we leave our estate to someone or something. Oh, I have a question for you. Do all dog treats have animal byproducts in them or would it only be a certain brand?"

"I haven't really studied it scientifically, but from what I know, unless it's an organic treat, all of them have animal byproducts in them. Why?"

"The fire department took a lot of samples of things from the carpeting and flooring at Maggie's house trying to figure out more about the fire. According to the chief, they found huge amounts of animal byproducts. His lab thinks it was from dog treats given to the dogs by Maggie's killer, so he or she could gain access to the house and commit the crime."

Jenna was quiet for several moments and then said, "That's interesting. I wonder if the dogs could identify the killer? A dog's sense of smell is so acute I'd think if they were exposed to the murderer, they would react in some form or fashion. Usually dogs sense humans they can't trust, and they indicate it by growling or some other hostile behavior, but in this case the fact that whoever it was gave them treats may cause them to react very positively to that person. I suppose it would depend on whether or not the dogs witnessed their owner being murdered."

"Kelly and I have a guard dog, and I trust his instincts completely.

However, if he'd been given a lot of dog treats, I don't know what would happen. Interesting situation. Jenna, it's late and I need to get home. Again, I'm really happy for the animal shelter. I can't think of a better organization to be the beneficiary of Maggie Ryan's estate. I'll be talking to you."

"Mike, thank you for being the bearer of good tidings. I think I need to go home and celebrate. This may just be the best day I've ever had."

"Don't know how long you've been married, Jenna, but when I caught three big trophy fish in one day in Cuba and told Kelly it was the best day of my life, she reminded me that I should have said the best day in my life was the day I married her. You might remember that," he said grinning as he walked out the door.

CHAPTER NINETEEN

"I'm home," Mike called out when he walked into the house from the garage. It was unnecessary, because all three of the Reynolds' dogs had immediately raced to the door knowing what his car sounded like. When Kelly heard their toenails bouncing on the hardwood floors she, too, knew Mike had arrived.

After giving each of the dogs a quick pat on the head he heard the sounds of pots and pans coming from the kitchen and figured Kelly was fixing dinner. "Hi, sweetheart," Kelly said without turning around. "I'll be with you in a minute. I just got home and need to start a couple of things for dinner. If I don't do it now, we won't eat until midnight, and that's way too late for both of us. Why don't you change your clothes, and then I've got a lot of things I want to tell you?"

"Will do, but I've got a few things to run by you as well. I'll be back in a minute," he said as he took a couple of dog treats from the cookie jar on the counter. "Come on guys, follow me. I've got a treat for each of you."

He returned a few minutes later followed by the dogs. "Kelly, can I ask you a question?"

"Of course, although you'd never needed my consent before."

"Well," he said sitting down at the kitchen table, "I've been wondering if the dogs really like me or do they follow me because of the treats I give them?"

"It's probably a little of both," she said diplomatically. "Lots of times they follow you around even though you don't have treats for them. I think they're pretty smart, but the sound of the lid being removed from the cookie jar might make them a little more prone to following you."

"Do you think we spoil them with too many treats?" he asked.

"Probably, but they really are good dogs, so I don't think we're hurting them by spoiling them. I really don't have a problem with any of them, although I will say it's nice that Skyy's outgrown the puppy stage of chewing on everything."

"Agreed. I'm exhausted, and could use a cup of coffee. If I make a pot will you drink a cup?"

"Sounds good. Want to tell me about your day or want me to start?" she asked.

"You start, and I'll make the coffee. So, what interesting things did you find out? Have a chance to talk to that principal friend of yours?" he said as he measured out the water and coffee. He pushed the start button and then gave his full attention to Kelly.

She came over to the table and sat down across from him. "Actually, Mike, I had quite a day. I'll start with Sunny. She came to the coffee shop as usual, and it was really crowded, like there were no seats for customers, but I wanted to talk to her, so I told her we could sit in the storeroom, and I'd have Charlie make her usual Cobb salad and she could eat there, which she did."

"Kelly, I know this may come as a complete shock to you, but I'm not particularly interested in what she had to eat. What I am interested in is whether or not you learned anything about the Ryan murder. Well, did you?"

"Yes," she said pouring each of them a cup of coffee, "and I think I have a suspect for you." She told him what Sunny had told her about Jimmy Richards and her suspicions that he might have abused his wife.

"Hmmm, that is interesting, although it's hard to believe that someone would carry a grudge that long and then act on it. And Kelly, while you know how strongly I feel about domestic abuse, I don't see where that ties into Maggie Ryan's murder."

"I know it's kind of carrying it to the next level, but I was thinking if someone is capable of domestic abuse, maybe they're also capable of committing murder."

"I dunno, Kelly, that's a pretty big leap, although in a convoluted way, I suppose it could be possible. I'll have to think about it. Tomorrow I'll call the superintendent of the Ocean Beach School District and see what I can find out about Allen Richards and his father, Jimmy, although he's the only suspect I have at the moment."

"I thought you were a little suspicious of the neighbor across the street. You mentioned you were going to talk to a couple of the other neighbors and see if there was bad blood between Maggie Ryan and the neighbor," she said standing up and walking over to the stove.

"I went to every house up and down the street, which wasn't very many considering the sizes of those lots. As you saw when you helped Jenna, it's kind of a funny neighborhood. There's several old farmhouses next to more modern houses that were built when the farmland around them was sold to people who wanted to build houses.

"Anyway, no one knew anything about either the neighbor I was suspicious of or Maggie Ryan. Guess both of them rarely went beyond their own property. I did pay another visit to the neighbor I was suspicious of."

"Find out anything?" Kelly asked as she stirred the beef and vegetable dish she was making in a large pot.

"Not really. The husband seems to be an okay guy, but the wife is another matter. From what I gather, she doesn't do anything but look out the window or watch television to see what's happening on the stock market. She's the type who even knows exactly when the mailman is going to be there. She said he should be there any minute, and she walked out the door with me when I left. The mailman pulled up in front of her house as I got in my car. She was right. He was there at 3:30 exactly.

"She mentioned again how much she hated the barking dogs and wasn't the least bit sorry Maggie Ryan was dead. Pretty harsh, but harsh enough that she could have committed murder? Although it's a stretch, I guess she could be considered a suspect.

"Shannon did tell me something of interest, but I have no idea how to follow up on it. She told me she'd seen a person, she was certain it was a man, walking down the street around the time of Maggie's murder. I asked all the other neighbors I talked to if they'd seen anything unusual that night, and all of them told me they hadn't."

"From the tone of your voice it sounds like you're not sure about that statement. Right?" Kelly asked.

"Here's what I'm struggling with, Kelly. On one hand the neighbor could be the murderer and made up the story about seeing someone walking down the street to deflect attention away from her. On the other hand, she could have seen the person who murdered Maggie Ryan, but how am I ever going to find out who that person is?"

"Let's take a break and eat. It's been a long couple of days for both of us. I've got more to tell you, so don't let me forget."

"Kelly, when you get involved in one of my cases, you're like a dog with a bone. You just hang on and won't let go. I don't think there's any way you'd ever forget something connected with one of my cases, and please notice I'm using the words 'my cases,' which I want to be very clear about. This is my case, not yours."

"Message received, Sheriff. I'm just going to tell you a couple of things I happened to learn today."

"Right, Kelly, right."

CHAPTER TWENTY

"I'll do the dishes, Kelly. You just sit there, look pretty, and talk to me."

"I'll sit here and talk to you, but as for looking pretty, think beauty is pretty much a matter of taste, and believe me, I'm glad that you have the taste you do. Okay, I just happened..."

"Kelly, whenever you say the words 'I just happened' I know there's a whole lot more to it, and how come things always seem to 'just happen' to you?"

"Don't know, Sheriff. Guess I'm just lucky, anyway, I told you I was going to the Cedar Bay Nursing Home with Rebel after work today. We went, and Roxie's neighbor absolutely loved Rebel. He was wonderful with her, and the director asked if we could come back next week, which we're going to do."

"Kelly, this is kind of like what Sunny had to eat for lunch. Is this about the Ryan case?" he said as he loaded the dishwasher with the rinsed dishes and began scouring the pots and pans.

"Getting there, Mike, getting there, just bear with me. The director asked if there was anything she could do for us, and I told her yes."

"What could she possibly do for you?" Mike asked as he turned around and faced her.

"Well, it's kind of a coincidence, and I know how you feel about them, but I prefer to think of it as karma, or something that was meant to be. When I talked to Sunny earlier in the day she told me Maggie Ryan had been friends with a retired teacher who was convalescing from a fall she'd taken and was a patient at the nursing home where Rebel and I had gone. Don't you think that's a coincidence, Mike?" she said smiling up at him. Her smile was returned by a raised eyebrow.

"And I'm sure Sunny just happened to mention that. I'm sure it wasn't in response to a question you'd asked of her."

"I really can't remember, and anyway, it isn't important. What is important is that the director introduced me to Linda Devine, Maggie's friend, and we had a long talk."

"I wouldn't have thought otherwise. And what did you just happen to find out?" Mike asked turning back to the sink.

"She used to take groceries to Maggie, and they talked a lot. She told Linda she'd been getting strange phone calls for some time. No one ever said anything, and then they hung up. She seemed to be frightened about them. Linda said it was about the time she started increasing the number of dogs she had. She thought Maggie was getting them for protection."

"I wondered about that, and it makes sense."

"She also told me Maggie had changed her will recently and seemed to be a little concerned about it, because Reverend Barnes still assumed he was going to inherit her estate."

"That fits in with what Lem told me when he called me after he'd met with Reverend Barnes. Evidently the reverend was in shock when he found out she'd changed her will. Lem said it was almost as if he personally needed the money. He told me that over the years he'd met with other organizations who'd been promised money by one of their members, but when he told them the member's will had been changed, they seemed to understand, and although they weren't thrilled about it, that was the end of it. He said that was not the case with Reverend Barnes."

"Well, since she was murdered before he found out about the will, that would probably mean he isn't a suspect. Would I be right?"

"Yes and no. Yes, he probably wouldn't be a suspect given the fact she was murdered prior to his finding out she'd changed her will. If he knew she'd changed her will, he might have killed her out of anger for what she'd done to him. But since he didn't know about the change, and he assumed he was still the sole beneficiary, there was no need for him to speed things up, so to speak, and take the risk of killing her. He could simply sit back, be patient, and eventually inherit her estate when she died of natural causes.

"On the other hand, no, he's still a suspect because of mistakenly believing he was the sole beneficiary of Maggie's estate. He may have murdered her in order to quickly get the money he desperately needed to pay off his gambling debts."

"Mike, are you saying he could have murdered her? I mean he's a reverend."

"Unfortunately, Kelly, people are human, and sometimes humans do bad things, professions notwithstanding."

"I had another thing happen that ties in with this."

"Kelly, Kelly, Kelly. I thought all you were going to do today, in addition to taking care of everyone at the coffee shop, was talk to Sunny."

"So did I, Mike, and honest, this was a complete coincidence, kind of one of those things you can't believe is happening."

"If you can't believe it's happening, that really causes me concern."

"Here's the deal, Mike. I stopped in at the market and happened to see a good customer of mine, Mary Price, she's the church secretary, and here's what she had to say." Kelly told him about her conversation with Mary.

"She told you she overheard the reverend saying 'It was all for nothing. I did it for nothing. She left everything to the animal shelter. I don't believe it.' Wow, that puts him pretty close to the top of the list of suspects. Sounds like he had a motive in that he needed a lot of money, and he needed it fast because he owed thousands of dollars to online gambling sites. Even if he had such a motive, I have nothing other than that to tie him to the murder. I wonder if I can get a photograph of him. Maybe there was a man walking down the street the night of the murder, and Mrs. Lewis could identify him, although she told me she didn't think she could," Mike said.

"I could ask Mary if she has a photograph of him for you, or you could probably go to the church's website and get one."

"Absolutely, emphatically do not ask Mary for a photograph. I'll handle this from now on. You are through doing anything else on this case. It's over for you."

"Okay, but will you tell me what's happening, at least? I really would like to know what's going on."

"Yes, I've told you before that although I don't like you involved in my cases, your instincts are often pretty good. Chief Rogers called me today. When his lab was going over more DNA evidence, they found a lot of animal byproducts. They even went back to the house today and vacuumed the carpeting and flooring. Evidently they found far more animal byproducts than would be normal, even when over thirty dogs were involved. He said it was strictly a theory, but he wondered if the killer knew about the dogs and brought a lot of dog treats so he or she could gain entrance to the house." He put the dish towel he'd been using on the rack and sat down across from Kelly.

"That would mean the killer knew there were a lot of dogs in the house, right?" she asked.

"Not only that, but it probably meant Maggie Ryan knew the killer. She might have even let him in and then the killer gave the dogs the treats or maybe he gave them to the dogs, closed the bedroom door, and killed her. That's just a theory. We really have nothing solid to back it up."

"Could the lab determine the brand of the dog treats?"

"No, I asked Jenna about that, and she said most dog treats have animal byproducts in them unless they're the vegetarian variety. By the way, when I gave the dogs a treat when I came home, I noticed that we're almost out of them. Might want to put that on your shopping list."

"Thanks. Since I'm not their primary treat giver, I hadn't noticed. I'll pick some up tomorrow. You mentioned Jenna. What's happening with her?"

"I think I told you Maggie Ryan left her entire estate to the Cedar Bay Animal Shelter. I went over to the shelter to tell her and she was thrilled. No, make that beyond thrilled, since she didn't know how she was going to keep it open because of the financial stress caused by the sudden influx of thirty dogs. I guess they'd been operating on a shoestring for quite awhile and the arrival of Maggie's dogs was about to put them under. It gave me a good feeling, and I'm sure if Maggie was alive, it would give her a good feeling, too."

"I'm so glad that at least something good has come out of all of this."

"I'd like to say I went over to the shelter to see Jenna for purely altruistic reasons, but to be honest I wanted to see her response when I told her," Mike said. "I know you're not going to like to hear this, but crime solving 101 teaches us that if someone or something is going to be the beneficiary of a will and a murder has been committed, that's where you start your investigation."

Kelly looked at him wide-eyed. "You can't seriously think that Jenna Lee had anything to do with the murder."

"No, I don't think so, but in a case like this I can't allow my emotions or personal feelings to affect my judgement on whether or not someone might have committed the crime."

"That's crazy, Mike. How could she have possibly known that the animal shelter would be the beneficiary of Maggie's estate?"

"I have no idea, but I'm just saying in a case like this I can't rule anything out, although she seemed to be both sincerely shocked and happy when I told her. Personally, I don't think she had anything to do with it, and I'd have to put her at the bottom of the list of possible suspects."

"I certainly hope you don't waste another minute going down that dead end, but Mike, something just occurred to me. The dogs were in the house when Maggie was murdered. I don't know how you could do it, but I wonder if one of them could ID the murderer."

"Nice thought, Kelly, but think about it. What would I do? Take each possible suspect and get thirty people to put thirty dogs or however many there are on leashes and then parade each of them by the suspects to see if there's a reaction. No, I don't see that happening."

"You're probably right. I just wish they could talk."

"So do I, sweetheart, so do I. I'm going into our office and do a little work. I'll join you in about an hour. Thanks for dinner. It was delicious, as usual."

"Thanks for cleaning up my mess. Love you, Sheriff."

"Ditto."

"Oh, Mike, one more thing. I don't know if I mentioned that one of the dogs that was at Maggie's was in pretty bad shape. It's a female German shepherd, anyway, when Jenna came to the coffee shop, and I told everyone about the dogs, Roxie and Jenna started talking. Dr. Simpson wanted to run some tests on the dog, and Roxie, her son, and her husband went over to see the dog, because her son had always wanted a German shepherd.

"Unfortunately, the X-rays showed she had a tumor. Dr. Simpson did a biopsy on it, and it's malignant. Roxie's beside herself, because they'd decided to adopt the dog if she was okay. Now she doesn't know what to do. Betsy, that's the dog's name, is being operated on in the morning. Roxie was thinking of going over to the veterinary clinic and waiting there during the surgery. Instead, I suggested she go over there when the surgery was completed, and Dr. Simpson should know something by then. I hope Betsy will be okay."

"Well, if anyone can help the dog, I'm convinced Dr. Simpson can. I think this little town is pretty lucky to have a vet of his caliber. When you find out anything, I'd like to know. Would you give me a call tomorrow?"

"Consider it done."

CHAPTER TWENTY-ONE

On her way to the coffee shop the following morning, Kelly hoped that because several days had gone by since Maggie Ryan had been murdered, the crowds at the coffee shop would taper off. It turned out to be a futile hope. There was a killer on the loose, and it made the townspeople of Cedar Bay nervous and they wanted to talk about it. Kelly's Koffee Shop was the logical place to go in the hopes that someone had news about it. No one knew anything other than what had been discussed for the last two days. Several people made comments that the sheriff should know something by now. It was very unsettling for Kelly.

She tried to allay the customers' fears with talk that Mike was getting very close to solving the murder, but she knew that was idle talk. From what he'd told her the previous evening, he was no closer to solving it than he had been just after the crime had been committed. She wished there was something she could do to help him, but nothing came to mind.

Promptly at noon the front door opened, and Doc walked into the coffee shop carrying a bulldog puppy with a bright red collar and a leash attached to it. Kelly rushed over to him and said, "Doc, this must be Max. He's adorable. I can see why you took him."

"He and Lucky are doing great. He seems to have accepted Max. I've been keeping him at the clinic with me in a wire kennel, so he can see me when I'm treating patients. Little guy follows me everywhere I go. Okay if I sit in that booth over there?" he asked. "I brought a couple of dog treats for Max, so I think he'll be fine sitting or lying down by my feet."

"Of course. If any food inspectors from the county come in, you can leave through the back door, but I don't think that will happen." She looked out the window and said, "I see Mike's patrol car pulling into the parking lot. Looks like you'll have company for lunch."

"Hi, sweetheart," she said to Mike as he walked in the door. "Roxie hasn't heard from Dr. Simpson yet, so that's why I didn't call you. Doc's in a booth at the back, and since he brought the newest addition to the Burkhart family, Max, you'll have a chance to meet him. He's absolutely adorable, and Doc says he and Lucky have become friends.

"Here's a menu for you and one for Doc as well. I didn't give a menu to Doc when he walked in, because I wanted to seat him in his booth as quickly as possible before someone complained about him having Max with him. I'll be over in a minute."

Kelly served several customers their orders and then walked over to the booth where Mike and Doc were sitting. "Well, gentlemen, anything look good to you?"

"We're going to make it easy on you and Charlie. We both want the blue cheese burgers, and we're going to split an order of onion rings," Doc said.

"You're the doctor here. You sure you two don't want something a little healthier. Mike, this kind of negates your healthy breakfast."

"That's exactly why I can justify it. I was so good at breakfast I deserve it," Mike said, "and Doc feels the same way. Right Doc?"

"Absolutely. Occasionally one has to indulge oneself, and I can't think of a better way to indulge than with onion rings and a burger."

"Okay, guys, it's your cholesterol, not mine. I'll place your order, and it should be up in a few minutes."

When she returned with their orders, Mike had Max on his lap and was gently petting him. "Doc, this little guy is really cute, and he seems extremely calm for a puppy. I remember when Skyy was a puppy, and she never stayed as still as this."

"Hope you don't mind, but I could use a little break, so I think I'll sit down with two of my favorite men," Kelly said as she served them their food, scooted into the booth, and sat next to Mike.

"Glad to have you, Kelly," Doc said taking a bite of his hamburger. "Tell Charlie this is perfect. Anyway, as far as why Max seems to be so calm, I did some research on the computer the night I got him and found out bulldogs are low energy dogs. One of the articles said they were great for older people and people living in apartments. In fact, it said if you wanted a dog to exercise with you, this was definitely not the breed to get."

"Looking at him right now, I think the article was right."

"Me, too. Another article I read said the breed can have a lot of health issues, so I took him in to see Dr. Simpson yesterday. Wanted a vet to look him over before I became so attached I couldn't help but spend thousands of dollars on him if he had some health problems. Fortunately, Dr. Simpson said he seemed to be in perfect health, and told me something that really surprised me."

"What was that?" Mike asked between bites of his onion rings and hamburger.

"He said this breed is pretty expensive to buy because the litter has to be delivered by caesarian section, and they can only be bred through artificial insemination. Takes quite a bit of money for an owner to have their dog bear a litter."

"That's bizarre," Kelly said. "I've never heard of that for any breed."

"Me neither. He told me they've been bred over the years to make their heads as big as possible. It's the mark of a good bulldog, but it also means that the heads are too big for natural birth. That's why the mother dog has to have a caesarian."

"Well, Doc, looks like you got an expensive dog for nothing, plus he's got a great temperament and is really calm."

"You might not have said that an hour or so ago."

"Why? What happened?" Mike asked.

"I had a couple of patients cancel their appointments, and the clinic was almost out of the latex gloves I use when I'm examining patients. I'd read that a new hospital supply store had recently opened near that subdivision south of town. I decided to drive down there and take a look at it. Never hurts to have a secondary place where you can get supplies. I found what I was looking for and as I was leaving, I noticed a hardware store nearby. I figured it would have a light bulb I needed for my garage."

"Did you take Max with you when you drove down there in your truck?" Kelly asked.

"Yes. I put a big box on the passenger seat and put him in it, but I probably didn't need to. As mellow as that little guy is he slept the whole time he was in the truck."

"So, if he was that mellow in the truck, what happened when he wasn't in the truck?" Mike asked.

"It was the darnedest thing I've ever seen. I took him into the hardware store. It's kind of one of those old-fashioned types that has about everything, and the owner knows where everything is. Anyway, I was walking over to a man I assumed was the owner and Max went nuts. He was yipping and trying to climb up the guy's pant leg. I couldn't believe it, because I've never seen him act like that. I couldn't calm him down. He just kept jumping up on the guy. At first the guy thought it was cute, but after a few minutes it was very clear he didn't like it. I finally picked Max up, bought the light bulb, and left. I still don't know what that was all about."

"Doc, do you remember the name of the hardware store?" Kelly asked.

"Yes, it was the AAA Hardware Store. I remember thinking at the time that the guy probably wanted to be listed first on the Internet, so that's why he chose that name for his store. I'm going to have to leave. Max has that 'I need to find some grass' look in his eye. Kelly, would you hold my bill, and I'll pay it tomorrow?" He quickly slid out of the booth and hurried out the front door.

"Mike, that's the name of the hardware store Jimmy Richards owns. Remember how I told you that both Sunny and the woman at the nursing home, Linda Devine, told me about that school incident with his son and Maggie Ryan. One of them, I can't remember which one, mentioned that he owned the AAA Hardware Store south of town."

"Yes, I remember you telling me about Jimmy Richards and Maggie Ryan, but I don't see where Max jumping on his leg and the school incident have anything to do with each other."

"Think about it, Mike. What if Jimmy Richards is the murderer, and he brought a lot of dog treats to gain access into the house. Maybe Max remembered his smell and associated it with the dog treats Jimmy had given him."

"That's a pretty big leap, Kelly. I don't think any court in the world would convict someone with evidence that flimsy. In fact, I don't think a three-month-old puppy would qualify as a star witness in a court of law."

"I know, but it sure is coincidental, and we both know how you feel about coincidences."

"True, but this may be one of the times when it was simply an exuberant puppy greeting a stranger. Think I'll take a pass on that theory, but thanks. I need to get back to work. The superintendent of the Ocean Beach School District was in meetings all morning, so I couldn't talk to her about Allen Richards. Her secretary said she'd be available this afternoon. See you at home," he said as he stood up and walked towards the door.

Kelly sat quietly for a few minutes, a plan developing in her mind. A plan she was certain would not be approved by Mike if she told him about it.

CHAPTER TWENTY-TWO

After Mike left the coffee shop, Kelly walked over to Molly and said, "I need to make a personal call. I'll be back in a couple of minutes."

She stepped outside the coffee shop, turned around, and looked at the front door where she'd taped the flyer Jenna had made about adopting or fostering one of Maggie Ryan's dogs. She pressed in the telephone number for the animal shelter, stepped away from the front door, and a moment later heard a voice say, "Cedar Bay Animal Shelter. May I help you?"

"Yes. I'd like to speak with Jenna Lee. Please tell her Kelly Reynolds is calling."

Within seconds Jenna was on the line. "Kelly, did your husband tell you the good news about the animal shelter being the beneficiary of Maggie Ryan's will? I still can't believe it. It's like all my problems have gone away. I am so happy. I've been so afraid we were going to have to close. I haven't been able to sleep at night thinking about what was going to happen to all the animals we have to care for that are here at the shelter."

"Yes, he did, and I think Maggie definitely made the right choice. I also saw the darling little bulldog Doc is fostering, although I'm sure you won't see him back at the shelter anytime soon. I have a strong feeling Doc will want to permanently keep the pup. Jenna, the reason I'm calling is I have a favor to ask of you."

"For you and Mike, anything. Just name it."

"It may seem a little strange, but were there any dogs among the ones that came from Maggie Ryan's that might be considered a guard dog breed?"

"We made a list of all the dogs we brought in from there, and the list includes the breed of each one. Let me look it over. Stay on the line, it might take me a minute."

While she waited, Kelly looked out at Cedar Bay, a view she never tired of. The sun was shining on the glassy expanse of water creating an effect of millions of bright, glittering diamonds as far as the eye could see.

"Are you there, Kelly?"

"I'm standing here just outside the coffee shop looking out at the bay. It really is a spectacular view. Okay, did you come up with anything?"

"Yes. Normally dogs that would be considered as guard dogs don't do well in a setting with large numbers of dogs, but I did find one. He's an Akita. Are you familiar with the breed?"

"I've never been around one, but I've seen photos of them, and I've seen them on television. I believe they were first bred in Japan and used as guard dogs. They're the ones with the curled over tails, aren't they?"

"Yes. They're very territorial animals, but surprisingly, they're great with children. They're quite large, so they can be intimidating. While I don't think of them as being in the same category as say a Rottweiler or a German shepherd, they are considered to be excellent guard dogs. I remember the one that came here from Maggie's group. He's a big boy, I'd say about one hundred pounds. Other than that, I don't much know about him. May I ask why you want to know?"

"I know this is going to sound really strange, Jenna, but I'd like to borrow him for a few hours. I can't adopt him, because we already have three dogs in the house. If it's okay with you, I'd like to pick him up about two-thirty this afternoon."

"Kelly, I'd love to say yes immediately, but I can't. I want to check him out and make sure he's not overly aggressive. I also want to see if he's leash trained. I don't want you to get hurt by a dog that's overly aggressive or one that pulls too hard on a leash. Give me a few minutes. I'll go out to the exercise yard right now and work with him a little. Do you want me to call you at the coffee shop or on your cell phone?"

"Better call me at the coffee shop. I usually don't carry my cell phone while I'm working. Thanks, Jenna. I'll look forward to hearing from you."

Kelly went back in the coffee shop and about twenty minutes later Molly motioned to her. Kelly walked over to Molly who was holding the phone. "You have a call," she said.

"This is Kelly Reynolds."

"Kelly, it's Jenna. I checked out the dog, actually one of the volunteers named him Sanyu, which means happiness in Japanese, and you can handle him with no problem. I'm a little concerned about why you asked for a guard dog, because I don't want anyone to get hurt. I hate to ask this, but could you assure me that you aren't planning on using him for something that might reflect unfavorably on the shelter."

"Yes, I can promise you that. I'll pick him up about two-thirty this afternoon and bring him back around six. How late will you be open tonight?"

"We're open until seven. See you later."

CHAPTER TWENTY-THREE

When Mike got back to the station his secretary handed him two telephone message slips. One was from the superintendent of the Ocean Beach School District, Leslie Moore, and the second one was from Jonas Goff, the manager of the Pet Friendly Store.

He got a cup of coffee and placed a call to the superintendent. "Ocean Beach School District. How may I direct your call?" the young sounding female voice asked.

"This is Sheriff Mike Reynolds returning Leslie Moore's call. I'd like to speak with her."

"Just one moment, Sheriff."

"This is Leslie Moore, Sheriff. Sorry I missed you this morning, but I was tied up in meetings. How can I help you?"

"Well, I don't know if you can. You may have heard that a retired Cedar Bay elementary school teacher, Maggie Ryan, was recently murdered, and I'm investigating the case. I understand the decedent had some problems with one of her students, a young man by the name of Allen Richards. From what I've learned, when Ms. Ryan wanted to hold him back from entering middle school, his father was furious, took his son out of the Cedar Bay School District, and transferred him to your district. Do you know anything about this situation?"

"More than I'd like to. The only reason I allowed Allen Richards to transfer here was because his father threatened to take his transfer request to the head of the Oregon Department of Education if I didn't grant permission for his son to transfer here. I should have followed my instincts and not accepted him. He was nothing but trouble from the moment he came. There were numerous instances of drug abuse problems with Allen, from showing up in class stoned to dealing drugs in school hallways. Fortunately, he dropped out of school after two years, and believe me, everyone but his father celebrated when that happened."

"I understand the father was in complete denial of any problems relating to his son. Was that your understanding as well?"

"That might be the understatement of the year. Jimmy Richards was by far the most difficult parent it's ever been my misfortune to deal with. I had to sit in on numerous meetings with him and various school personnel. He was belligerent, threatening, and blamed his son's teachers and the educational system in general for failing to teach his son. I heard that after Allen dropped out of school he spent time in several drug rehabilitation facilities, but none of them seemed to help his drug addiction problem."

"I've not met either of them, nor have I seen any photographs of them. Could you give me a physical description of both of them? I find it helps me in my investigations if I can visualize them in my mind. He's not a suspect in the case, but from everything I'm hearing, he's definitely becoming a person of interest."

"Sheriff, I can do better than that. I can send you a picture of both of them. When you called this morning, you told my secretary that it was in reference to Allen Richards, so I pulled his file. I'm looking at photos of both of them as we speak. Would you like me to fax their photos to you?"

"Yes. Here's my fax number," he said. "One last question, and then I won't take up any more of your time. Have you or anyone else in the school district heard from Jimmy Richards since Allen dropped out of school?"

"I haven't, and I think I would have been told if anyone else had. I know Jimmy Richards has a hardware store in that new development just south of Cedar Bay, but that's all I know about him. Believe me, I'm just glad I don't have to deal with him anymore. When you have to deal with a parent like him, you can't help but feel sorry for his child, and quite frankly, it doesn't surprise me that Allen turned out as he did. It was kind of a given once you met his father."

"I appreciate you taking the time to talk to me. If you happen to think of anything else about him, I'd like to know. Thanks."

CHAPTER TWENTY-FOUR

After he finished speaking with Leslie Moore from the Ocean Beach School District, Mike called the Pet Friendly Store and asked to speak with Jonas Goff. He was told that Jonas was on a break, but the person who answered the phone said he'd go into the employee's rest area and get him.

A few minutes later a man said, "This is Jonas Goff. May I help you?"

"Jonas, this is Sheriff Reynolds. I'm returning your call."

"Thanks, Sheriff. This may be absolutely nothing. I'm the manager of the Pet Friendly Store. We're in that new shopping center just south of Cedar Bay. I was watching TV last night, and I saw on the news about the woman who was murdered and that she'd had over thirty dogs living on her property. Naturally, anything having to do with dogs interests me.

"This is a real long shot, but I got to thinking about how anyone could get into a house and murder someone when there were over thirty dogs in the house. I'm a murder mystery fan. Matter of fact, think I've read about every murder mystery around, and I particularly like the ones with dogs in them. Anyway, a while ago I read one about how a murderer had gotten into a house by giving dog treats to the two dogs that lived in the house. You know how it is, Sheriff, your mind starts rambling, and I remembered that one of my employees told me she'd sold three big bags of dog treats to a man.

I'm talking about really big bags of dog treat. Each bag weighs ten pounds, so this guy bought thirty pounds of dog treats. Sort of strange, don't you think? My employee told me because after the man left she got to wondering how many dogs the guy was going to give them to. You with me?"

"I think I am. If I'm following you, you're telling me you wonder if one of your employees sold dog treats to the person who murdered Maggie Ryan. Is that what you're saying?"

"I'm not accusing anybody of anything, but you have to admit it's pretty strange when a customer buys three large bags of dog treats, and then a woman is murdered, and she has over thirty dogs. Don't know if there's a tie-in, but after I saw it on TV I thought I'd give you a call."

"I don't know either, Jonas, but I'd like to talk to your employee. Would that be possible?"

"She's here now, but her shift is over at 5:00. We don't close tonight until 10:00. Any chance you could come over now?"

"I'm on my way. I'll be there in about half an hour, and thanks. Don't know where this will lead, but it's definitely worth looking into."

Twenty-five minutes later Mike pulled up in front of the Pet Friendly Store which was located in a strip mall catering to the residents and pets of the nearby residential development. There was a cleaners, hair salon, drug store, Thai restaurant, private mailbox store, and a pet store at the end of the small neighborhood mall.

When Mike entered the store, a man walked over to him and said, "You must be Sheriff Reynolds. I'm Jonas Goff. We can go back to my office. I told Missy Logan, she's the one who sold the man the pet treats, that you were coming and wanted to talk to her."

They walked to the back of the store and Jonas opened a door that had the words "Manager" written on it. Mike followed him into the small room. A young woman sitting in a chair looked up at him and said, "You must be the sheriff. I'm Missy Logan, but I don't know why Jonas wanted me to tell you about the man who bought the dog treats."

Mike sat down in the chair next to her and said, "Missy, a woman was recently murdered, and she had a lot of dogs in her house. We're looking at anything that might help us identify her murderer. When someone buys a large amount of dog treats, and there's a lot of dogs at the scene of the crime, it may have something to do with the murder. I'd like you to tell me everything you can about the person who bought them."

She looked down at her hands and then up at Jonas. "Missy, please, tell the sheriff what you know. Why don't you start with when you sold the treats to him?" Jonas said.

"Well, it was last Saturday. I remember because I was going out on my first date with Lenny. He's a big deal at my school. That's how I know it was Saturday. It was late in the afternoon, and this man had a shopping cart with three big bags of dog treats in it. I asked him how many dogs he had, and he said he didn't have any, but his friend had a lot. That's about it. He paid and left."

"What did he look like?" Mike asked

She thought for several moments and then said, "I'd say he was about your height. He had a medium build, you know kinda normal, like he wasn't real buff or anything. He had dark hair. He was dressed in casual clothes, jeans, and a shirt. I don't remember what color his eyes were."

"Thanks," Mike said, "that helps. Do you remember if he was young or old?"

Again, she was quiet while she thought. "I'd say he was about my dad's age. He's forty-four."

"Do you think you'd recognize him if you saw a picture of him?"

"Probably, because I've thought about him a lot. It was weird that anyone would buy that many dog treats."

Mike opened the file he'd brought with him. "Missy, do you recognize either of these two men? Did one of them buy the dog treats from you?"

Mike had copied a photo Reverend Barnes had posted on the church's website, and he'd brought that photograph and the one of Jimmy Richards that the district superintendent had faxed to Mike earlier that afternoon. Missy examined both photographs carefully and then looked up at Mike and said, "Yes, that's the man who bought them. I'm positive." She pointed to one of the photographs.

"Thank you, Missy. I really appreciate you taking the time to talk to me," Mike said as he put the photographs back in his file.

"Sheriff, can you tell me anything more about this?"

"I'd rather not say right now, Missy. If I find out something, I'll be in touch with you. Again, thanks for your help."

"Missy, you can go back to work now," Jonas said. She stood up and he closed the door behind her. "Well, Sheriff, what do you think?"

"I think your time reading those mystery novels, particularly the ones with dogs in them, might help to break this case. While I still can't prove that the man who bought the dog treats killed Maggie Ryan, it's a good start. Thanks for calling me. I'm sure you were a little nervous I might discount your instincts."

"You got that right, Sheriff. I figured I didn't have much to lose other than you laughing when I told you. Glad you found it worth your while."

"I certainly did. Jonas, I'd like you to keep this quiet. Would you ask Missy to do the same? I have a feeling I'm getting close to solving this case, and I don't want any problems with it."

"No problem. Consider it done. Anything else I can do for you?"

"Yes. My wife would never forgive me if I was in a pet store and didn't get something for our three dogs. Anything you particularly recommend?"

"We just got a new product in last week. I bought one for my dog, and it's now her favorite thing. She goes to her toy box first thing in the morning to get it. Let me get three of them for you."

He stood up and walked out the door with Mike following him. He turned down an aisle marked "Chew Items" and stopped before a bin with what looked like some type of animal horns in it.

"What are these?" Mike asked as Jonas handed him three of them.

"These are small pieces of elk horns, and for some reason dogs love them. Please take them as a thank you for the service you do for our community. A gift from me to you. Missy's at the cash register. I'll tell her it's on me and walk you to the door."

"Thanks, Jonas. You've just made three dogs very happy."

Mike got in his car and started the engine, then took a moment to see if there were any messages for him on his phone. He was surprised to see that Shannon Lewis had called him and said she'd remembered something from the night of the murder.

He turned off his engine and pressed her number into his phone. It was answered almost immediately by her. "This is Shannon Lewis, is that you. Sheriff?"

"It is, but how did you know it was me?" he asked.

"I don't get many calls, so jes' figured you was returnin' my call. You told me to call ya' if I thought of somethin'. Well, I did. Remember how I tol' ya' I'd seen what looked like a man walkin' down the street? I remembered it 'cuz I thought it was pretty strange that he'd be pullin' a cart, but in all the excitement I forgot to tell you the part 'bout him pullin' some little cart behind him.'"

"I agree. That's pretty strange. What kind of a cart was it, Shannon?"

"I don't exactly know what they're called, but ya' ever been to the Sunday swap meet over in Portland?"

"No, I haven't. Why?"

"Cuz you woulda seen all kinds of carts like the one he had at the swap meet. People put the treasures they buy in the carts and pull the carts behind them. They're made outta some kind of a fencin' like material."

"Do you mean mesh?"

"Yeah, but it's not a fine mesh. More like a fence, if ya' know what I mean. 'Scuse me fer a minute. Ralphie's jabberin' at me." A moment later she came back on the phone and said, "Ralphie says to tell ya' it's a wire cart. Now ya' know what I'm talkin' 'bout?"

"I think so. Shannon, I have a couple of photos I'd like to show you. Do you think you could identify the man you saw in the street if you saw a photo of him?"

"Save the taxpayer's dollar on gas, Sheriff. Ain't no way I could identify him. We ain't got no streetlights here, and it was dark. It was a new moon kind of night. All I saw was what looked like a man pullin' a cart behind him. Got any thoughts why someone would do that?"

"No, I need to think about it. All right, Shannon, if you're certain you can't identify anyone, I won't bother to come over. I really appreciate you calling me. I'm not sure how the cart figures into all of this. Often it's a matter of just accumulating a lot of information and then it becomes very clear. Tell Ralph hello and again, thanks."

A cart. That's interesting. I don't quite see the nexus if the guy she saw was the killer. I'll tell Kelly tonight. Maybe she'll have some ideas.

CHAPTER TWENTY-FIVE

Kelly parked her minivan in front of the Cedar Bay Animal Shelter and walked in. The door to Jenna's office was open, and she waved for Kelly to come into her office. "Sanyu's all ready for you to take him. I've been out to see him several times since you called, and he's a love. I'd feel better if you'd tell me what you have planned, but knowing you're a dog lover, I'm certain it's nothing that will cause a problem for Sanyu."

"No. I just want to take him a couple of places and see what his reaction is to some people. I promise that nothing will happen to him. Do I need anything?"

"No, here's his leash. He was fed this morning, and I personally took him on a walk just a little while ago. I can assure you that you won't have to worry about him going to the bathroom while you have him unless you're going to be gone longer than a couple of hours."

"I think we'll be back before then. I do have kind of a strange request, though. Do you have any therapy dog wraps? You know, the kind that goes around their middle and says 'Therapy Dog in Training' or 'Therapy Dog' on it?"

"I don't think I want to know anything about this, Kelly, but yes, I do have one. I'm assuming you want it for Sanyu, would I be right?"

She opened the drawer of a nearby file cabinet and handed a therapy dog wrap to Kelly.

"Yes, I want it for him. Since he knows you, would you mind putting it on him? Thanks, Jenna, and when I come back I'll tell you all about this."

"I'm going to hold you to that, because my curiosity is really aroused."

Jenna stood up and walked around her desk. "Sanyu knows me by now, so I'll introduce you to him. Follow me." She led Kelly out of the main building and down a long walkway with covered small kennel-like rooms on each side. Halfway down the walkway she stopped and said, "This is where Sanyu's staying. I'll go in and put him on the leash." Kelly watched while Jenna easily slipped the leash catch into the metal clip on his collar, attached the therapy dog wrap around him, and walked him to the door. "Sanyu, meet Kelly. She's going to take you for a ride."

Sanyu was a beautiful specimen of the Akita dog breed. He was fawn and white with intelligent eyes that seemed to size up Kelly as she held her hand out to him, palm down. After a few moments of examining her, he sniffed her hand and evidently decided she'd passed whatever test he had silently given her. What it had consisted of, she had no idea, as he stood in front of her and looked up.

During a lull at the coffee shop earlier that afternoon, Kelly had done a little research on the coffee shop computer about the Akita breed and learned they automatically assumed the dominant role in any relationship unless a dog or person had more of an alpha personality than they did. She stood at her full height and said in a very firm voice, "Sit, Sanyu," as she took the leash Jenna handed to her. The big dog immediately sat down, and she reached down and patted him on the head.

"Come, Sanyu," she said waving to Jenna as she walked to her minivan with him next to her. Since there were no records as to where he'd come from, she could only assume that whoever had owned him prior to Maggie Ryan had spent a lot of time training him. She wondered why anyone would have given him up and decided it was probably not a decision the previous owner had much choice in. When they got to the minivan he sat and waited while Kelly opened the car door. "In, Sanyu," she said. He jumped into the minivan and sat down in the passenger seat.

When she put her seatbelt on, the big dog began to nose his seatbelt and talk to her in a dog growl. "Sanyu, do you want me to put the seatbelt on you?" she asked, feeling stupid.

He yipped, and she fastened it around his middle. He immediately looked out the windshield, obviously ready for the ride. It was a short trip to the Church of Loving Grace. Kelly wanted to see what Sanyu's reaction would be to Reverend Barnes. She just hoped he'd be at the church. She got out of her minivan and walked around to the passenger side, opened the door, and unhooked Sanyu's seatbelt. She lightly pulled on his leash and said, "Come, Sanyu."

She entered the church building and walked down the hall leading to Mary's office. The door was open to Reverend Barnes' office, and she saw him sitting at his desk.

"Hi, Reverend Barnes. How are you?"

"Fine, Kelly. What brings you to our church? And who is this guy?" he asked as he walked around his desk. "I see he's a therapy dog. Are you working with an organization that trains therapy dogs? And is it okay if I pet him?"

"Sure, you can pet him, and no, I'm not working with any organization. I'm just helping a friend. Sanyu, sit."

Kelly watched intently to see what the dog's reaction would be to Reverend Barnes. She was ready to yank on the leash if the dog became hostile towards the reverend. He put his hand down and let Sanyu smell it. A moment later he petted the dog, who sat quietly. There was no reaction from Sanyu, positive or negative, other than sniffing the reverend's hand. Kelly was certain the reverend wasn't the one who had given dog treats to Maggie Ryan's dogs.

"Sweet dog, isn't he, Reverend? To answer your earlier question, I ran into Mary yesterday at the market, and she mentioned she had a great stew recipe. I forgot to ask her for it, so I thought we'd stop by and see if I could get it. Is she in?"

"That's a very nice dog. I'm not familiar with that breed, and in answer to your questions about Mary, she is here. She's getting us some coffee and should be back any minute."

"Hi, Kelly. What a nice surprise to have you stop by the church. Here's your coffee, Reverend. Kelly, come on into my office, and who is this beautiful boy?"

"Well, I don't know if you can call a male dog beautiful," Kelly said. "Maybe handsome would be a little better," she said laughing. "We came to get that stew recipe you mentioned yesterday. Winter's coming, and I think a stew would work well at the coffee shop." They went into Mary's office, and she closed the door.

"I wanted to tell you that the Reverend said he wants to talk to me, and he's coming over for dinner tonight. Kelly, I'm so nervous. I don't know what to expect."

"Mary, I think I can assure you he isn't the murderer. He may have some gambling problems, but you can work with that if you want to. Do you?"

"Yes, I've made up my mind that if he wants me to help him, I will, but I don't have any frame of reference for this."

Kelly put her hand on Mary's shoulder. "Mary, just do whatever your heart tells you. It usually knows a lot better than we do what the answer is, and keep in mind that even though we don't see each other that often, I'd be happy to listen if you ever want to talk about it."

"I'll send you the recipe and give you a call tomorrow. I just have to get through tonight, and then I'll probably know where this is going to lead, if anywhere. He may be coming over to tell me he's firing me, and he never wants to see me again."

"Somehow I don't think that's it. Sanyu and I need to leave. We have two other stops to make before I have to take him back, and Mary, the reverend looks a lot better than what I thought he'd look like, given our conversation of yesterday."

"I know, he does look a little better today, but I just wish I knew more."

CHAPTER TWENTY-SIX

Kelly parked her minivan a block down the street from Shannon Lewis' house, looked at her watch, and smiled. Her timing was perfect. It was 3:28 and from what Mike had said after he interviewed her, Shannon Lewis always went out to her mailbox at exactly 3:30 in the afternoon to get her mail when the mailman delivered it.

"Okay, Sanyu, I'll release your seatbelt, put you on a leash, and then let's see how this one goes. Come on, boy."

Kelly and Sanyu began walking on the sidewalk towards Shannon Lewis' house. *Come on, Shannon. Open the front door and walk out to your mailbox. If I have to turn around at the end of the street and come back this way, we're going to look very suspicious. Come on.*

When they were thirty feet from the Lewis mailbox, Kelly saw the front door of the Lewis house open and a portly grey-haired woman walked out of it and headed towards her mailbox. Ten feet from where the woman was getting her mail out of the mailbox Kelly said, "Sanyu, sit." The dog sat looking up at Kelly. The woman turned towards Kelly and said, "That's a mighty big dog. What's up with that funny tail?"

"He's an Akita, and that's just the way their tails are. I didn't want him to frighten you, so I gave him the command to sit."

123

The woman walked over to where Kelly was standing and said, "I'm not much on dogs, but he's a purty one. Old woman who died across the street used to have a bunch of 'em. You may have read about it in the paper or seen it on TV. Dogs were barkin' night and day. Darn near drove me crazy, but yours hasn't made a peep. Mind if I pet him?"

"No, he's friendly. Just put your hand in front of him, palm down, so he can smell you first. If he licks your hand it means he'd love to be petted." Kelly held her breath while Shannon Lewis put out her hand, and Sanyu licked it.

That's the second of the three suspects I have in mind that have passed the test. Don't know if it would hold up in a court of law, but I'm convinced she isn't the murderer. Time to visit the third suspect and see if he passes the test.

"Nice dog. I've read a lot about therapy dogs like him. Guess they do a lotta good. Mind you I ain't getting' a dog, but he might be first if I ever did. Got some stock market information here I need to read. Nice talkin' to ya'." She turned and went back into her house. Kelly and Sanyu turned around and walked back to the minivan.

"Nice job, Sanyu. Here's a treat for you," she said as she opened her glove compartment and pulled out a dog cookie. "Good boy."

She drove to the freeway and headed south, pulling off on Chapman Avenue. She'd looked up the address of AAA Hardware Store on the computer at the coffee shop earlier that afternoon and easily drove to it.

"Okay, Sanyu, let's see how you do with this one. If nothing happens here, I'll never again act on one of my 'off the wall' crazy theories." She took a deep breath and walked through the door of the hardware store.

"May I help you?" the dark-haired man wearing jeans asked. Sanyu immediately moved closer to Kelly and sat down, refusing to move, as a low deep growl came out of his throat. "Some therapy dog, Miss, if he growls at a stranger. Have you been training him for very long?"

"No. He was one of the dogs that belonged to a woman who was murdered a couple of days ago," she said, carefully watching his reaction to that statement.

Sanyu continued to growl. "Easy, boy, easy," Kelly said gently petting him. An angry yet fearful look quickly passed over the man's face as he concentrated his attention on Sanyu. He looked up from Sanyu to Kelly as if he was trying to place her. Now that she'd seen Jimmy Richards in person she remembered he'd been in the coffee shop several times, and she wondered if he recognized her.

"I need a new watering can for my plants. My old one sprang a leak, but I think I better come back another time, without him. We're just starting his therapy dog training, and obviously, it's not going well. See you later," Kelly said brightly. "Sanyu, come." The big dog stood up but suddenly snarled and leaped forward towards the man. Kelly yanked on his leash and held it tightly as she struggled with some difficulty to keep him in check while they made their way out of the hardware store and back to her minivan.

That was Kelly Reynolds, the owner of Kelly's Koffee Shop. She's married to the sheriff that's handling the murder investigation. I saw him on the news being interviewed about it, and I'd swear that was the same dog I had all the problems with when I was in the old lady's house. I remember that curled tail. Darned near didn't make it out of there because of him. She or the sheriff, or maybe both of them, must be suspicious of me.

She must have brought the dog here to see what his reaction, if any, would be to me, and it certainly wasn't good. I wonder how much they know? Wish I could leave the store and go home, but I've got a delivery coming any minute. It's a cash delivery, and I've got to be here to pay for it when it's delivered.

Trash truck comes to the house tomorrow, but that might be too late. Sure wish I'd never put those empty bags that had the dog treats in them in the trash barrel behind the house. I was worried when I put them in there that Amanda would see them and wonder why they were there. Now it looks like her seeing them is the least of my problems.

Kelly took Chapman to the freeway and drove north. Kelly's mind was spinning.

There is no doubt in my mind that Jimmy Richards is the murderer. If Sanyu could talk, I know he would identify him, but if I tell Mike what I just observed, although he may agree with me, he'll tell me no District Attorney in his right mind would charge a man with murder on evidence that flimsy.

I'm sure he must have given the dogs treats, so they'd be distracted while he killed Maggie Ryan. He would have needed a lot of treats, and Mike said they found a lot of residue from the treats in the house. So, how did he get rid of the bags? He could have put them in a bin in some shopping center parking lot, but he would have risked being seen. I'll bet he put them in his own trash barrel at his home.

"Sanyu, we're going to the coffee shop and rest for a little while. I'll give you some water, and I bet I can find a special treat for you. Then when it gets dark you can come with me to the Richards' house. Kind of interesting that although everything seems to be done on computers these days, a lot of people still list their addresses in an old-fashioned telephone book. I'm sure I can find it. Are you okay with doing that?" The big dog barked, and she was sure he'd understood every word she'd said.

CHAPTER TWENTY-SEVEN

Mike was on his way home when the phone in his car rang. "This is Sheriff Reynolds."

"Sheriff, it's Brandon. We just had a call that I thought might be of interest to you. A man called in and said he'd seen you on the television interview you did earlier today when you were asking people to call the station if they knew anything about the murder. You also mentioned that over thirty dogs were in the house and if anyone knew anything about that to call."

"Go ahead. I'm heading for home. Do I need to stop by the station on the way?"

"You can decide after you hear this. Here's the thing. This guy was jogging with his dog around 6:30 the night of the murder. He told me he and his dog always run the same route which includes looping around a local neighborhood shopping center. When they got to the back of the shopping center he saw a man dressed in black opening the trunk of his car. He said it stuck in his mind because he thought what was in the trunk was really strange."

"I'll bite," Mike said. "What was in it?"

"The guy said there was a wire cart, kind of like you sometimes see senior citizens use at the supermarket, plus there were several huge empty bags in the trunk of his car. It looked like this guy was getting ready to throw the empty bags in a trash dumpster next to his parked car, but here's the real kicker. The empty bags were for a certain type of dog treat. The bags have a distinctive color and logo on them, and the jogger recognized the brand because it's the same brand of treats he gives his dog. When the man spotted the jogger, he closed the trunk, and sped away without throwing anything in the dumpster. He didn't think much about it until he saw you on TV. What do you think?"

Mike was quiet for a few long moments as the pieces of the puzzle began to fit together in his mind. "Brandon, did he say what the guy looked like or if he could identify him?"

"Yes. The guy was in his mid-forties, about six feet tall with dark hair. He was wearing jeans. The jogger said he got a very good look at his face, and he'd be able to identify him."

"Brandon, I'm pulling over, and I'm going to send you a photograph of a man. Call the jogger back and send it to him. See if it's the same man and get back to me immediately. I also want you to get Judge Hilken's phone number. I may need him to issue a search warrant. I'll wait for your call."

Within minutes the phone in Mike's car rang. He saw Brandon's name on the screen. "What did you find out, Brandon?"

"It's the same guy. He positively identified him. Here's Judge Hilken's home number as well as his number at the courthouse. What do you want me to do?"

"Stay where you are. I'll be at the station in a few minutes. I want you to call the trash company and see what day they pick up trash at Jimmy Richards' home. His address is in the Ryan file on my desk." Mike called the judge on his way to the station and convinced him that although he had quite a bit of circumstantial evidence, he needed a search warrant for Jimmy Richards' home and premises. The judge told him he'd grant it, and Mike could pick it up at the judge's home in about half an hour.

Mike drove to the station, picked up Brandon, and headed for the judge's home. "Brandon, what did you find out about the trash pick-up?"

"Tomorrow is the scheduled day for that neighborhood. Why, do you think this Richards guy has something in his trash?"

"If you were surprised putting something in a shopping center trash bin, wouldn't the logical place for you to get rid of it be to put it in your own trash barrel at home?"

"Yeah, I guess it would. So, are we going to do a trash barrel dive? I'm not quite dressed for that."

"I don't know exactly what we're going to do, but my gut feeling tells me we're on the right track, and I've learned to trust it."

"Well, from what I saw at the murder scene in that house, I hope your gut is right."

CHAPTER TWENTY-EIGHT

After stopping at Judge Hilken's home and picking up the search warrant he'd authorized, Mike and Brandon drove to the street where Jimmy Richards lived and easily found his home. It was a tired looking house badly in need of some tender loving care. They drove down the street, turned right, and then made another right to see what was behind the house. After Mike had picked up Brandon, he'd driven his patrol car to his house and exchanged it for his van. He didn't know what to expect, but a patrol car was a dead giveaway that law enforcement personnel were looking at something in the neighborhood.

The Richards home backed up to an empty lot which was unfenced, and the back yard of the Richards home didn't look much better than the vacant lot. Weeds took the place of grass, and no attempt had been made to make it attractive. There were several abandoned cars parked in the empty lot along with all sorts of urban trash. Although it was quite dark, Mike could see that the only things separating the Richards' back yard from the empty lot were three large trash barrels belonging to the Richards home.

Mike pulled into the empty lot and exclaimed, "What the blazes…" He abruptly stopped his van when he saw Kelly's minivan parked in the vacant lot with an Akita dog sitting in the passenger seat with the window rolled down. The big dog looked at Mike briefly and then directed his attention back to the area of the trash barrels.

"Something wrong, Sheriff?" Brandon asked in a whisper.

"Yes. The minivan over there is my wife's. She has a tendency to get involved in my cases. I have no idea what the dog is doing sitting inside her minivan. Open your door as quietly as you can…"

As he was saying that the back door of the Richards home flew open, and Jimmy Richards came charging out of the house brandishing a gun and yelling, "Get out of that trash barrel, Kelly. I know you figured everything out. I'm going to take care of you just like I took care of Maggie Ryan."

Mike stood next to his van and yelled, "Drop your gun. Police."

At that moment, the big dog in Kelly's minivan jumped out of the open window, ran towards Richards, who was looking in Mike's direction, and leaped on him, causing him to drop the gun in his hand and knock him to the ground. When the gun hit the ground it harmlessly discharged with a loud bang. Sanyu stood over him, snapping and snarling in a threatening manner, his huge open mouth only inches from Jimmy Richards' throat.

"Mike, I'm over here," Kelly yelled. Mike ran towards her and yelled for Brandon to handcuff Jimmy.

"Kelly, what in the devil are you doing here? I didn't even see you."

"I heard a car drive onto the lot, and I didn't want to be seen by anyone, so I hid between two of the trash barrels. I was having a hard time getting the lid off of one of the barrels, and I think Jimmy heard it."

"Are you all right?" he said squatting down to where she was sitting on the ground and wrapping his strong arms around her.

"I'm fine Mike. I'm so glad I brought Sanyu with me. I think

Jimmy would have killed both of us. Mike, I found three large empty dog treat bags in one of the trash barrels, and when Sanyu and I went to Jimmy's hardware store..."

"You what? Never mind. We'll talk later. Right now, I need to take care of Jimmy." He called the station and asked for two back-up deputies. He walked over to where Jimmy was laying on the ground with the big dog standing guard over him. "Kelly, would you call this dog off? I think between Brandon and me we have the situation under control."

"Sanyu, come." The big Akita walked over to where Kelly was sitting on the ground and sat down next to her. She patted his head and said, "Good boy, Sanyu, good boy."

"Jimmy Richards, I'm arresting you for the murder of Maggie Ryan," Mike said.

Just then the back door to the house opened and a woman wearing a nondescript dress with grey-blond hair walked out. "What's going on out here? I was watching television when I heard shouting and what sounded like a gunshot. Jimmy, what are you doing laying there on the ground?"

"Amanda, tell them I was home the night of the murder of that old woman who had the dogs. You know I was. We were watching television together after dinner. Remember?"

Amanda Richards quickly assessed the situation and realized her worst fears had just come true. Her husband was the person who had murdered Maggie Ryan because of an incident that had occurred over ten years earlier. She looked down at Jimmy and then looked over at Mike. "Sheriff, Jimmy's lying. He was gone from the house about the time I read in the paper that Maggie Ryan was murdered. If you need me to testify, I will. The only good thing to come out of this is that he won't be beating me up anymore."

Mike's two backup deputies raced up to the house in a patrol car and ran into the back yard. "Take him down to the station and read him his Miranda rights. Brandon and I will be there shortly." He walked over to the trash barrels and said, "Kelly, which one has the dog treat bags in it?"

She pointed to the one in the middle and then said, "They're under one of those carts like older people use at the supermarket. You know, people pull them along behind them."

"Yes, and that means Shannon Lewis was right. She did see the murderer, Jimmy, dragging a cart behind him. Just wish she could have seen him well enough to identify him. Brandon, get a couple of large evidence bags out of my van and put the cart and the empty dog treat bags in them. We need to take them to the station and log them in as evidence."

He walked over to where Sanyu was sitting by Kelly and patted the big dog on the head. "Kelly, I thought we'd agreed on no more dogs. Where did he come from?"

"Mike, it's a long story. A really long story, but he's not mine. I'll take him back to where he belongs just as soon as I leave here, I promise."

"You do that, and I'll see you at home later, and Kelly, I'm glad you're all right," he said as he pulled her up from where she was sitting on the ground.

"Me too."

CHAPTER TWENTY-NINE

"Hi, Jenna," Kelly said as she and Sanyu walked into the animal shelter after they'd driven there from the Richards home. "I can't thank you enough for loaning Sanyu to me. I wish I could keep him, but Mike is adamant that three dogs in our household is enough."

"I have no idea why you wanted to borrow him, but I'm glad I could help."

"Actually, Sanyu was responsible for saving my life as well as Mike's, and he helped Mike catch Maggie Ryan's murderer."

"What?" Jenna screamed. "What are you talking about?"

"It will probably be on the news tonight and in the paper tomorrow. Sanyu is a real hero. Matter of fact, you may have some reporters here pretty soon. I would imagine there are going to be a lot of people who'll want to adopt Sanyu when they hear about it, so you better get ready for them as well. I've got to get home. It's been a long day." She walked over to Sanyu, knelt down, and said, "Thank you for saving our lives, big fella. I don't think the case would have been solved without you." She stood up, waved goodbye to both of them, and walked out the door.

I know it sounds ridiculous, because people consider me to be a good cook, but all I want tonight is comfort food. I'm going to make us hamburgers along with macaroni and cheese. Might even have a chocolate sundae for dessert.

When she got home she changed her clothes, fed the dogs, prepped the food for dinner, and waited for Mike. She was dreading the coming conversation she knew she was going to have with him. An hour later she heard his car pull into the garage, and she mentally braced herself.

"Hey, everybody, I'm home. Kelly, where are you?"

"I'm in here. Mike, before you get mad at me I want to explain what happened."

"That would be nice, considering I felt like I'd been blindsided when I saw your minivan in the empty lot with a dog I didn't recognize inside it."

She told him everything that had happened from the time he'd left the coffee shop after lunch to when she'd seen him at Jimmy Richards' home. She explained how she was convinced, after the conversation with Doc and hearing how Max had reacted to Jimmy, that the murderer could be identified by a dog. She said she was pretty sure it was Jimmy, but since there were two other solid suspects, she needed to make sure. Once she'd seen Sanyu's reaction to Jimmy, she knew her theory about the dog treats, along with the evidence found in the house, was solid.

"Mike, honest, I was just trying to help. I was really sure that if I could find the dog treat bags, along with Sanyu's behavior towards Jimmy, it would be enough for you to arrest him. I would have made it if it hadn't been for the noise from the trash barrel lid I had trouble getting off. Please don't be angry with me," she said, looking at him as innocently as it was possible for her to look.

"Kelly, I'd be less than honest if I told you that I wasn't angry with you, but the reason I'm angry with you, and the reason I don't want you involved in my cases is that you almost got killed tonight. If it hadn't been for that dog and me showing up at the right moment, I'm not sure what would have happened to you. Just the thought of

135

what could have happened to you makes me sick with worry."

"But Mike, you have to look at the positive side. I'm here, and you caught the killer. That's pretty much a win-win in my book, but I would like to know how you happened to show up at the exact moment I needed you."

"I know, Kelly, you're a glass half-full person, and that's one of the things I love most about you. As to how I got there when I did…" He related the chain of events that had happened that afternoon, concluding with getting the search warrant from the judge.

"Well, I think we've both had enough excitement for one day. I'll make you a deal, actually it's a deal we pretty much do every night. I'll cook if you clean up, and then I'm going to bed."

"Deal, and I'll be right behind you."

She'd just turned the oven on when her cell phone range. She looked at the monitor and saw it was Roxie. "Roxie, I hope you have good news about Betsy."

"The best, Kelly, the best. Dr. Simpson says he was able to remove the entire tumor, and she's going to be fine. He even did some more biopsies on the surrounding tissue and they were all benign. We had to promise we'd keep her quite for awhile, but we get to bring her home in three days. I'm so excited I can hardly stand it."

"Enjoy your evening, Roxie, and I'll see you in the morning."

"How come you didn't tell her about what you were up to tonight?" Mike asked.

"I wanted her to just have this evening to celebrate. I'll tell her about it tomorrow, and I'm sure it will be the main topic of conversation at the coffee shop."

"Of that I have no doubt," Mike said.

CHAPTER THIRTY

Kelly was right. The following day was as busy at the coffee shop as the previous ones had been with everyone wanting to talk to Kelly about her part in apprehending Maggie Ryan's murderer. The night before, just as she and Mike were finishing up dinner, the press had come to their home, taken photographs, and fed their interview to the area television stations. The story was on all of the late news channels and there were pictures of Kelly, Mike, and Sanyu. The local newspaper had run a front page story that morning about how Jimmy Richards was apprehended, including a big photograph of Sanyu. Kelly and Mike figured it had been a slow news day.

"Kelly, Jenna Lee is here. She says she can't stay for lunch, but she wants to talk to you for a minute."

"Thanks, Molly." Kelly walked over to the coffee shop entrance where Jenna was standing with a big mile-wide grin on her face.

"Kelly, I can never thank you enough."

"For what?" Kelly asked.

"Because of the television coverage and the article in the newspaper this morning, we've placed eighteen of the Maggie Ryan dogs. With the other dogs that were already placed, that leaves only five that haven't found homes yet, and I'd bet they'll be taken before the end of the day. Everyone wants to have a dog that was around Sanyu. The press was at the animal shelter just after you left last night and again when I got there early this morning. They took all kinds of photos of him and the shelter. I imagine he'll be on the news again tonight."

"Was Sanyu one of the dogs who was adopted?" Kelly asked thinking of the big Akita who had fearlessly rushed to protect her and no doubt saved her life.

"Kelly, it was unbelievable. In addition to the press, there was a line of people waiting to adopt him this morning. I had to do a first come, first serve type of thing."

"So who is the lucky new owner of Sanyu?" Kelly asked.

"It was a woman by the name of Shannon Lewis. She said she'd met you and him yesterday when you were on a walk. I figured I was better off not knowing any more than that, but she and her husband, Ralph, were thrilled to have him. He's home with them now."

"You're kidding. I'm absolutely blown away. She lives across the street and down from Maggie Ryan's home and said she hated the barking that came from there. She gave me the impression that a dog would be the last thing in the world she'd ever want."

"Nope, and they were very happy to get him. They said they'd never had a dog before, which is surprising given their ages. It's pretty rare for people to get their first dog when they're older. Anyway, I just want you to know how much good you've done for the shelter."

"My pleasure. Glad I could help. You and the shelter provide a needed service. Excuse me, but I better get back to work. Roxie's waving at me."

She walked over to where Roxie was standing and saw Mary Price sitting at a small table. "Mary, I didn't see you come in. How are you?"

"You were so busy I didn't want to interrupt, but if you have a minute, I'd like to talk to you."

"Of course," she said sitting down across from Mary. "What did you want to tell me?"

"Well, I'll make a long story short and simply tell you that Reverend Barnes and I are getting married, and he's going to start attending Gambler's Anonymous meetings. He worked out an arrangement with the online gambling sites to pay them back in installments over an extended period of time. I told him I wanted to make sure he was sincere about quitting gambling, so we won't be getting married for six months. This coming Sunday during his sermon he's going to tell his congregation addiction. He intends to tell them that he's as human as they are, and no one is absolutely pure."

"Mary, I'm so happy for you. That's wonderful news."

"What I haven't told him, Kelly, is that I inherited quite a bit of money from my parents when they died as well as when my husband died. My parents were the type of people who never spent an unnecessary penny for anything. As a matter of fact, I can remember how we always used paper napkins until they were shredded, and only then could we get another one.

"Sorry, I'm digressing. Anyway, I've been very lucky with my investments, and if he keeps his word, I'll pay off his debts when we get married. He has no idea that I have any money, so I know he's not marrying me for it. I decided that would be my wedding present to him. The money needed to pay off his gambling debts is just a little bit of what I have."

"Mary, I wish you both the best. Everybody has something they have to deal with, and both of you are going to be well aware of what you'll be dealing with when you get married. That's a good way to start out a marriage. Please give Reverend Barnes my best wishes. I'd love to talk to you, but since it's standing room only in here, I think I'll lose my help if I stay and talk to you any longer."

Kelly walked away from the table with a big smile on her face, feeling that for the moment, everything was good in the little town of Cedar Bay.

RECIPES

PECAN MONKEY BREAD

Ingredients:
1 package of frozen bread dough (I use the dough that is used to make rolls.)
1 cup brown sugar, packed
6 tbsp. unsalted butter, cubed, plus additional for greasing pan
½ cup unsalted butter, melted
6 tbsp. heavy whipping cream
6 tbsp. chopped pecans, divided
1 cup sugar
1 tsp. ground cinnamon

Directions:
Preheat oven to 350 degrees. Grease a bundt pan with butter. (I've also used a springform pan with a small ovenproof bowl in the center, but the bundt pan works much better.)

Put the brown sugar, cream, and cubed butter in a pan and bring to a boil. Cook for 3 minutes, stirring often. Pour ½ of the mixture into the bundt pan and sprinkle with ½ of the pecans.

Mix the sugar and cinnamon together.

Divide the dough into 40 pieces and form into balls. Roll the balls in the melted butter and then in the cinnamon sugar mixture. Place 20 balls in the bundt pan and pour half the brown sugar mixture over them. Sprinkle with half of the pecans. Place the final 20 balls in the bundt pan, pour the remaining brown sugar mixture and pecans over them. Cover with plastic wrap and let rise for 30 minute at room temperature. Bake for 40 – 45 minutes or until the top is a golden brown. Cool for 10 minutes. Invert onto a serving plate and serve warm. Enjoy!

NOTE: This recipe was sent to me be one of my readers, Thomas Palmer. I used frozen dough in place of making the dough from scratch which his recipe called for.

SAVORY MONKEY BREAD

Ingredients:
1 package frozen bread dough (I use the dough that is used to make rolls.)
8 tbsp. unsalted butter, melted
8 oz. grated parmesan cheese (I usually buy it already grated, but if you're a purist, you can certainly grate it yourself.)
2 tbsp. dry Italian spice (You can be creative with this and use any combination of spices you like.)
1 tbsp. garlic salt

Directions:
Preheat oven to 350 degrees. Place the butter in a small dish with sides. Stir together the cheese, spices, and garlic salt and place on a plate or in a dish. (I've been known to put it all in a big plastic bag and coat the balls that way.)

Divide the dough into 40 pieces and roll into balls. Roll the balls in the melted butter and then coat them with the cheese mixture. As each one is coated put it in a bundt pan or springform pan with a small ovenproof bowl in the center. (The bundt pan works much better.)

When all the rolls are in the baking pan, put plastic wrap over the top and let it rise for 30 minutes. Bake 30 – 40 minutes. (Ovens vary and the kind of pan you use can affect the cooking time, so keep an eye on it. Cool for 10 minutes. Invert onto a serving dish and serve.) Enjoy!

PESTO STUFFED PORK CHOPS

Ingredients:
2 bone-in 1 ¼ inch thick pork chops
1 tsp. black pepper
1 tsp. dried oregano
1 tsp. minced garlic
¾ tsp. salt
½ tsp. crushed red pepper flakes
1 tsp. ground thyme
2 tbsp. balsamic vinegar
1 cup pesto sauce (I buy a jar at the store – if you have a Costco in your area, I think theirs is the best.)
1 cup bread crumbs (You can use packaged, but I like to make mine by brushing olive oil on small shredded pieces of bread and sprinkling them with garlic salt. I toast them in the oven at 375 degrees for 10 – 12 minutes.)

Directions:
Preheat oven to 375 degrees. With a thin sharp knife, cut a deep slit in the side of each chop to make a pocket that extends to within ½ inch of the bone. Combine pepper, oregano, garlic, salt, red pepper flakes, and thyme and rub both sides of each chop with the mixture.

In a small bowl combine the pesto sauce and the bread crumbs. Stuff the pesto mixture into the pork chops and secure with tooth picks. (I use a lot of tooth picks!) Place the chops in a shallow ovenproof dish and bake for 30 minutes. Remove from the oven, brush the chops with balsamic vinegar, and bake for 5 more minutes. Plate and serve. Enjoy!

Embarrassingly Simple Side or Topping

Ingredients:
1 pint coleslaw (I get mine from the deli section at the supermarket.)
½ mango, peeled, and cut in small ½ inch cubes

Directions:
Combine the coleslaw and mango in a bowl and chill in the refrigerator for 30 minutes. If serving as a side dish, put in small individual ramekins or on a plate. If serving as a topping, put the mixture in a bowl and let your guests serve themselves. Enjoy!

NOTE: This is soooo simple, it's hard to believe it's as good as it is. It's wonderful on pulled pork sandwiches, tuna steak sandwiches, chicken sandwiches, or hamburgers. Trust me, the possibilities are endless, and once you start serving it, you'll find there's very little that doesn't go well with it!

APPLE CLOUFITIS

Ingredients:
½ cup all-purpose flour
1/3 cup plus 2 tbsp. sugar
¼ tsp. ground cinnamon
Pinch salt
3 eggs, plus 1 egg yolk
1 cup whole milk
½ tsp. vanilla extract (Use real extract. It makes a difference.)
2 tbsp. unsalted butter
1 ½ cups peeled, cored, and diced apples
2 tbsp. sugar
1 tsp. of a fruit liqueur such as apple brandy (Optional)
Powdered sugar for dusting
1/3 cup whipped cream

Directions:

Preheat oven to 350 degrees.

Batter: Sift flour, sugar, cinnamon, and salt into a bowl. In a separate bowl whisk the eggs, egg yolk, and milk until well blended. Add about 1/3 of the egg mixture to the flour mixture and whisk until smooth. Gradually incorporate the remaining egg mixture into the flour mixture until well blended. Cover with plastic wrap and refrigerate while preparing the apples.

Apples: Place butter in an ovenproof 10-inch cast iron or stainless steel skillet and cook over moderate heat until butter turns brown. Add a pinch of salt and the apples. Cook, stirring often, until the apples are slightly softened, about 2 minutes. Sprinkle sugar over the apples.

Reduce the heat to low and cook until the apples are almost cooked through, and the sugar has melted, coating the apples in a light syrup. Take the pan off the heat and add the liqueur. Place back on heat and swirl the pan slightly.

Spread the fruit evenly in the pan. Pour the batter over the fruit and bake in the oven about 15 minutes or until the edges of the cloufitis are browned and the center is set. Ovens vary so you may have to adjust the amount of cooking time.

Remove from the oven and put some powdered sugar in a sieve and dust the surface of the cloufitis with it. Serve warm directly from the skillet with a dollop of whipped cream.

Paperbacks & Ebooks for FREE

Go to www.dianneharman.com/freepaperback.html and get your FREE copies of Dianne's books and favorite recipes immediately by signing up for her newsletter.

Once you've signed up for her newsletter you're eligible to win three paperbacks. One lucky winner is picked every week. Hurry before the offer ends!

ABOUT THE AUTHOR

Dianne lives in Huntington Beach, California, with her husband, Tom, a former California State Senator, and her boxer dog, Kelly. Her passions are cooking, reading, and dogs, so whenever she has a little free time, you can either find her in the kitchen, playing with Kelly in the back yard, or curled up with the latest book she's reading.

Her award winning books include:

Midlife Journey Series
Alexis

Cedar Bay Cozy Mystery Series
Kelly's Koffee Shop, Murder at Jade Cove, White Cloud Retreat, Marriage and Murder, Murder in the Pearl District, Murder in Calico Gold, Murder at the Cooking School, Murder in Cuba, Trouble at the Kennel, Murder on the East Coast, Trouble at the Animal Shelter

Liz Lucas Cozy Mystery Series
Murder in Cottage #6, Murder & Brandy Boy, The Death Card, Murder at The Bed & Breakfast, The Blue Butterfly, Murder at the Big T Lodge

High Desert Cozy Mystery Series
Murder & The Monkey Band, Murder & The Secret Cave, Murdered by Country Music, Murder at the Polo Club

Midwest Cozy Mystery Series
Murdered by Words, Murder at the Clinic

Jack Trout Cozy Mystery Series
Murdered in Argentina

Coyote Series
Blue Coyote Motel, Coyote in Provence, Cornered Coyote

Website: www.dianneharman.com
Blog: www.dianneharman.com/blog
Email: dianne@dianneharman.com

Newsletter

If you would like to be notified of her latest releases please go to www.dianneharman.com and sign up for her newsletter.

63340098R00096

Made in the USA
Lexington, KY
03 May 2017